P9-CFD-481

"Sawyer gives us something rare in this age of the quotidian hero: a genuine tragedy. It is no accident that he invokes Greek myth in the title of the book. Sawyer is willing to play on the same field as Aeschylus and Euripides, and he proves himself equal to the task. JASON is, in my opinion, the deepest computer character in all of science fiction. And Aaron is, in my opinion, one of the most well-drawn, fallible, *human* detectives I've encountered in mystery fiction—in a league with [Ruth] Rendell's Inspector Wexford. You might as well buy two copies in the first place—one to read and keep, and one to shove at your friends, saying, 'Read this! Now!' How good is *Golden Fleece*? A friend of mine—an English professor—used to ask, whenever he saw me, 'Why are you still writing that spaceship stuff?' Now I can answer. Because *this* is possible."
—Orson Scott Card, *The Magazine of Fantasy and Science Fiction*

"A well-paced page-turner replete with hard science."
—*Quill & Quire*

"An elegant spacecraft mystery; a compelling tale of deception that relies more on sociology than technology."
—*The Toronto Star*

"Suprising and ingenuous."
—*Locus*

"Suspenseful, entertaining, inventive, thought-provoking, and funny. I enjoyed this one a lot. Highly recommended."
—*Mystery Scene*

"Like reading *Jaws* from the shark's point of view. *Golden Fleece* is a refreshingly different science-fiction mystery with a double-wham conclusion in the style of *Twilight Zone*."
—*The Niagara Gazette*

"The writing is smooth and the reading effortless. The characters—even JASON—evoke your sympathy. I'm looking forward to what Sawyer does next."
—*Analog*

NOVELS BY ROBERT J. SAWYER

*Golden Fleece**

*Far-Seer*

*Fossil Hunter*

*Foreigner*

*End of an Era*

*The Terminal Experiment*

*Starplex*

*Frameshift**

*Illegal Alien*

*Factoring Humanity**

*Flashforward**

*published by Tor

ANTHOLOGIES EDITED BY
ROBERT J. SAWYER

*Tesseracts 6* (with Carolyn Clink)
*Crossing the Line* (with David Skene-Melvin)

# GOLDEN FLEECE

## ROBERT J. SAWYER

TOR®

A TOM DOHERTY ASSOCIATES BOOK
NEW YORK

GOLDEN FLEECE

Copyright © 1990 by Robert J. Sawyer.
Revised edition copyright © 1999 by Robert J. Sawyer.

A novelette version of this book appeared as the cover story "Golden Fleece" in the September 1988 issue of *Amazing Stories* magazine.

Edited by David G. Hartwell

A Tor Book
Published by Tom Doherty Associates, LLC
175 Fifth Avenue
New York, NY 10010

www.tor.com

Tor® is a registered trademark of Tom Doherty Associates, LLC

Design by Lisa Pifher

Library of Congress Cataloging-in-Publication Data

Sawyer, Robert J.
    Golden fleece / Robert J. Sawyer.—1st ed.
        p.   cm.
    "A TOR book."
    ISBN 0-312-86865-0 (acid free paper)
  I. Title
PR9199.3.S2533G65     1999
813'.54—dc21                                                    99-37454
                                                                     CIP

First Edition: November 1999

Printed in the United States of America

0  9  8  7  6  5  4  3  2  1

For my parents,
John A. Sawyer
and
Virginia Sawyer

# ACKNOWLEDGMENTS

This novel would not have taken flight without the help and encouragement of Algis Budrys, Dr. R. W. Bussard, Richard Curtis, Terence M. Green, Patrick Lucien Price, Dr. Ariel Reich, Brian M. Thomsen, and especially Carolyn Clink.

Many thanks to Ralph Vicinanza, David G. Hartwell, Jim Minz, and Tom Doherty for arranging for the publication of this revised edition.

Beta testers for *Golden Fleece* were Ted Bleaney, David Livingstone Clink, Franklin R. Haber, Mark C. Petersen, Alan B. Sawyer, and Andrew Weiner. Any remaining bugs are my own.

# GOLDEN FLEECE

# THIS IS YOUR CHANCE TO GO INTO SPACE!

## THE UNITED NATIONS SPACE AGENCY
## REQUIRES
## PEOPLE FROM ALL WALKS OF LIFE
## FOR
## FIRST EXTRASOLAR PLANETARY SURVEY

We require 10,000 people to form the crew of *Argo*, first in UNSA's Starcology (space-traveling arcology) series of Bussard-ramjet starships. Starcology *Argo* will conduct a complete survey of Eta Cephei IV ("Colchis"), a verdant, Earthlike world 47 light-years distant. True to the Starcology community-in-space idea, we will consider workers in all realms of human endeavor. Applicants must be under 30 years of age and in good general health. [R]eply to this posting and an application will be downloaded to your terminal.

# ONE

I love that they trusted me blindly. So what if it was ship's night? For centuries, astronomers had labored while others slept, and even if there was no way to see outside during our long voyage, Diana Chandler still hadn't broken the habit of not starting work until after I had dimmed the lights in the corridors.

I'd suggested to Diana that she might be able to verify her startling findings by using some of the equipment stowed in the cargo holds. That no one had been down to the lower decks for almost two weeks didn't seem to bother her. That she was alone in the middle of my artificial night fazed her not in the least. After all, even with 10,034 people on board, I'm sure she felt safe as long as she was under my watchful eyes. Indeed, she seemed perfectly calm as she headed into a service corridor, its walls lined with blue-green algae behind acrylic sheets.

I'd already wiped the files that contained her calculations

and notes, so there was just one more loose end to tie up. I slid the door shut behind her. She was used to that soft pneumatic hiss, but her heart skipped a beat when it was followed by the *snick-snick* of spring-loaded locking bolts sliding into place.

Up ahead, a rectangle of red light spilled onto the sod from another open doorway. She walked toward it. Her paces were measured, but signs of nervousness were creeping into her medical telemetry. As soon as she passed through that door, I closed and locked it, too.

"JASON?" she said at last, her normally sunny voice reduced to a tremulous whisper. I made no reply, and eleven seconds later she spoke again. "Come on, JASON. What gives?" She started walking down the corridor. "Oh, be that way if you must. I don't want to talk to you, either." She continued to march forward, but the tappings of her heels concatenated into a rapid rhythm that matched her racing heartbeat. "I realize you're upset with me, but, well, you'll just have to trust my judgment on this." I quietly winked off the lighting panels behind her. She looked back, down the blackened corridor, then continued forward, her voice quavering even more. "I *have* to tell Gorlov what I've discovered." Wink. "The people on board have a right to know." Wink. "Besides, you couldn't have kept something like this secret forever." Wink. Wink. Wink. "Oh, shit, JASON! Say something!"

"I'm sorry, Diana," I said through speakers mounted on the crisscrossing pink metalwork of the ceiling. Those words were enough to tell Di that the crazy fears running through her head were *not* crazy, that she was very much in trouble.

Dilating the valve on the pipe made a pleasing reptilian sound. Diana laughed nervously, found the strength for a final attempt at humor. "Don't hiss at me, you rusty heap of—" She gagged as the chlorine hit her. Covering her mouth with her sleeve, she ran, pounding on door after door. Not that one. No, not yet. Just a few more. On your left, bitch. Ah—*swoosh!* She burst into the cargo hold and the door slid shut behind her. I snapped on the wall-mounted spotlights. The floor was a simple open grating: the pink metal of the artificial-gravity field generators, bare of any covering. Through the small triangular openings made by the metal intersections she could see level after level of storage compartments, each filled with aluminum crates.

She scrambled for one of the steel bars used to lever the lids off these crates and—"Damn you, JASON!"—smashed the splayed end into my wall-mounted camera unit. Shards of glass cascaded to the floor, falling on and on through the open gratings. Undaunted, I swiveled an overhead camera pair to look down on her. This angle foreshortened her appearance. From here she didn't look like an entirely adequate astrophysicist, a shrewd collector of antiques, a recently separated but passionate lover, or—by all accounts—a great cook. No, from here she looked like a little girl. A very frightened little girl.

Di's wrist medical implant told me that her heart was pounding loudly enough to thunder in her ears. Still, she must have heard the electric hum of my overhead camera swiveling to track her because she turned and hurled the metal bar at that unit. It fell short, bouncing with a *whoomp* on the lid of a crate. For a moment, she stared up into my camera eyes, horror and betrayal plain on her face. Such an attractive woman: her yellow hair separated so well from the shadows. Given the lighting in the hold, she could probably see her own reflection, a fun-house parody of her fear, spread wide over the curving surface of my twin lenses.

She ran on, but stopped again to evaluate her alternatives when she came to a four-way intersection between rows of crates. As she stood, she fingered the tiny pewter cross she wore on a chain around her neck. I knew it was her mannerism when she was nervous. I knew, too, that she wore the cross not for its religious significance—her Catholicism was nothing but a field in a database—but because it was more than three-hundred years old.

She decided to run down the aisle to her left, which meant she had to squeeze past a squat robot forklift. I set it after her, the antigravity force from its pink metal base lifting it four centimeters off the floor. As it hummed along after her, I let loose a blast from its horn. I looked at her now from the forklift's point of view, seeing her from behind. Her hair bounced wildly as she ran.

Suddenly she pitched forward, tumbling onto her face. Her left foot had caught in the open floor grating. I cut power to the forklift's antigravs, and it immediately dropped back to the floor a few meters behind her. It wouldn't do to crush her here. She got up, epinephrine surging, and took off down the corridor with two-meter strides.

Ahead was the hatch I'd been shepherding her toward. Di made it through into the vast hangar deck. She looked up, desperate. Windows into the hangar control room, thick panes of glass, began ten meters above the floor and covered three sides of the bay. They were dark, of course: it would be six subjective years before we would arrive at Colchis, where the ships stored here would be used.

On either side of the hangar were twenty-four rows of silver boomerang-shaped landing craft, the nose of one ship tucked neatly into the angle of the next. Names mostly associated with the Argonauts of myth were painted on their hulls.

Ahead was the plated wall that separated the hangar from vacuum. Diana jumped at the sound of groaning metal. The wall jerked loose in its grooves, and air started hissing out.

Di's hair whipped in the breeze, a straw-colored storm about her head and shoulders. "No, JASON!" she shouted. "I won't say anything—I promise!" Foolish woman. Didn't she know I could tell when she was lying?

A thin stripe of deadly black appeared at the bottom of the hangar's outer wall. Di screamed something, but the rising roar drowned her words. I swung a spotlight onto the lander *Orpheus*, its outer air-lock door open. That's right, Diana: there's air inside. The wind fought her as she climbed the stepladder into the tiny, lighted cubicle, the growing vacuum sucking at her back. Her nose had begun to bleed from the sudden drop in pressure. Grabbing the manual wheel in both hands, she forced the lock to cycle. When she was safely within the body of the lander, I slid the hangar wall all the way up.

The view of the starbow was magnificent. At our near-light speed, stars ahead had blue-shifted beyond normal visibility. Likewise, those behind had red-shifted into darkness. But encircling us was a thin prismatic band of glowing points, a glorious rainbow of stars—violet, indigo, blue, green, yellow, orange, and red.

I fired *Orpheus*'s main engines, a silent roar in the vacuum, clouds of greenish gold exhaust billowing from the twin cones. The boomerang lifted from the deck and moved with gathering speed across the expanse of hangar and through the open space door.

My remote cameras inside *Orpheus*'s cockpit focused on Diana's face, a mask of horror. The telecommunications link crackled with static—radio-frequency interference from the ramfield. As soon as the lander darted past the overhang of the ramscoop funnel, Diana's body would begin to convulse: the hard radiation pelting into it would scramble her own nervous system. Almost instantly she would undergo cardiac arrest and her brain, its neurons firing spasmodically for a few seconds, would cease to function.

The feed from my remote cameras flared brightly for an instant as the lander roared out into the sleet of hydrogen ions, and then the picture died. The communications link had given out before Diana's body had. A pity. It would have been an interesting death to watch.

# TWO

MASTER CALENDAR DISPLAY • CENTRAL CONTROL ROOM

| | |
|---|---|
| STARCOLOGY DATE: | MONDAY 6 OCTOBER 2177 |
| EARTH DATE: | SUNDAY 18 APRIL 2179 |
| DAYS SINCE LAUNCH: | 739 ▲ |
| DAYS TO PLANETFALL: | 2,229 ▼ |

aron, we have an emergency. Wake up. Wake up *now*."

It was an autonomic response for me, completed before I could even think of halting it. In retrospect, I'm hard-pressed to say which of my algorithms initiated my locator program first. Aaron's job, although he hadn't had a lot to do so far, was supervising Starcology *Argo*'s fleet of landing craft. Certainly there was a hard-coded directive that required him to be notified immediately of any accident involving those ships. But Aaron, by coincidence, had also recently ended a two-year marriage contract to Diana Chandler. There was a next-of-kin routine that would seek out the closest relative of anyone injured or killed. That Aaron was, by virtue of their divorce, no longer Diana's next-of-kin had probably invoked a judgment circuit to resolve the inconsistency. That would have delayed the decision to contact him on those grounds for a few nanoseconds, likely allowing the job-related summoning of him to trigger my speakers first.

Next to Aaron lay Kirsten Hoogenraad, M.D., eyes closed but wide awake. Something had been interfering with her sleep of late. Perhaps it was simply that she was unused to sharing a bed, at least for the purpose of getting rest. In any event, she jumped at the sound of my voice and, propping herself up on one elbow, shook Aaron's shoulder. Normally, I bring up the lights slowly when someone is waking, but this was no time for gentleness. I snapped the overhead panels to full illumination.

Aaron's EEG shuddered into consciousness, whatever dream he had been having dissolving as wave fronts cascaded together. I spoke again. "We have an emergency, Aaron. Get out of bed quickly."

"JASON?" He rubbed yellow crystals from his eyes. Implanted on the inside of his left wrist was my medical sensor, which doubled as a watch. He squinted at its glowing digital display. "You mystic! Do you know what time it is?"

"The lander *Orpheus* has just taken off," I said through twin speakers on the headboard. That did it. He rolled out of bed, flat feet slapping the floor, and stumbled across the room to retrieve his pants from where he'd left them, tossed in a heap with one leg inside out.

There was no point in telling him to hurry. His heart was beating somewhat erratically and his EEG made clear that he was still fighting to wake up. An inefficient boot-up procedure if you ask me.

"Please call an elevator," said Aaron, his voice dry and husky. That's what he gets for sleeping with his mouth open.

"I already have one waiting," I said. Kirsten was ready to go, pulling the belt of her blue velour robe tight at her waist. The action accentuated the lines of her figure.

I slid both the bedchamber and main apartment doors aside, the hisses of their mechanisms rising and falling quickly. Kirsten darted down the corridor and entered the waiting lift, quite unnecessarily putting her hand on the rubber molding along the edge of the open door as if to keep it from closing. Aaron thundered along the hallway and joined her.

The car began its fifty-four-level drop. The elevator itself operated silently, running on pink antigrav motors in a vacuum shaft. But I always whistled a descending tone through my speakers when the cylindrical cabs were going down and an ascending tone when they were going up. It had started as a joke: I'd expected someone to realize that the damned things should have been silent. So far, seventy-three million elevator rides to my credit, no one had noticed.

Aaron looked up at my paired cameras, mounted above the elevator door. "How did it happen?"

"The ship was appropriated," I said, "for reasons unknown."

"Appropriated? By whom?"

No easy way to say this. It was too bad Kirsten had to be there. "Diana."

"Diana? *My* Diana?" Kirsten's face was blank—a carefully controlled blank, with muscles bunching in their attempt to show no expression. Her medical telemetry told me that she was stung by Aaron's use of the word "my." "Can you contact her?" he asked.

"I've been trying since the moment she left, but there's too much interference from our ramfield." The elevator popped open, revealing one arm of the U-shaped hangar-deck control room. Aaron and Kirsten rounded the corner into the crosspiece of the U. Clustered around the instrumentation consoles were the dozen others I had summoned, mostly clad in pajamas and robes. Seated at the center of the group were tiny Gennady Gorlov, the mayor of Starcology *Argo*, looking about as disheveled as Aaron did, and giant I-Shin Chang, chief engineer, clad in one of those specially tailored denim jumpsuits he required to accommodate his four arms. Chang had been off working on his secret project, instead of sleeping, even though this was his normal sleep period.

Aaron peered out the observation window that ran along the inner walls of the control room, overlooking three sides of the hangar. His eyes fixed on the still-open space door. "Distance to *Orpheus?*"

"Fifty klicks," said Chang in his staccato delivery. The engineer vacated the chair in front of the main console, its cushioned seat rising ten centimeters with a pneumatic hiss. He gestured with his lower left hand, not quite as beefy as its upper counterpart, for Aaron to take his place.

Aaron did so, then stabbed a finger at the central view-screen, a glowing rectangle cutting the observation window into two long curving panes. "External!"

I produced a holographic rendering of Starcology *Argo.* The principal material part of our Bussard ramjet looked like a wide-mouthed bronze funnel. At this level of resolution, the great reticulum of field wires extending outward from the funnel was invisible. Girdling the inside of the funnel cone halfway down was the magnetic torus; girdling the outside at the same location was the windowless ring-shaped habitat, painted a sea green in color, its plated walls looking like a sheet-metal quilt. Most of the remainder of *Argo's* three-kilometer length was a cylindrical silver shaft, interrupted here and there by gold and black tanks and compressors. At the end of the shaft was the tight cluster of cylindrical igniters, the bulbous, copper-colored fusion chamber, and the corrugated, flared fusion-shield assembly. In front of *Argo,* I added a tiny silver angle-bracket representing the runaway lander.

"*Orpheus's* velocity?" asked Aaron.

"Sixty-three meters per second and slowing," I said through the speaker on the console before him.

"She's moving perpendicular to the ramfield's magnetic lines of force, yes?" said Chang, the words coming out of him like machine-gun fire. "That's dragging her down."

"Will *Orpheus* collide with us?" asked Mayor Gorlov.

"No," I said. "My autonomic meteor-avoidance system angles the ramfield away from us whenever a metallic object enters it. Otherwise, *Orpheus* would have hurled down the funnel and destroyed our ramjet."

"We need that ship back," said Gorlov.

"That *ship?*" Aaron swiveled his chair to face the little man. The underscoring squeak of its bearings made his exclamation sound shrill. "What about Di?"

The mayor was twenty centimeters shorter than Aaron, and massed only two-thirds what he did, but there was nothing tiny about Gorlov's voice. I often had to run a convolution algorithm on it to clear out distortion. "Wake up, Rossman," he bellowed. "It's suicide to enter the ramfield." Gorlov's campaign had not been won on the basis of his gentle manners.

Kirsten laid a hand on Aaron's shoulder, one of those non-verbal gestures that seemed to communicate so much for them. Her touch did have a slightly calming effect on his vital signs, although, as always, the change was difficult to measure. He squeaked back to face the viewer and scooped a calculator off an adjacent console, cupping it in his palm. I swiveled three of my lens assemblies to look at it, but none of them could make out what he was typing.

"*Orpheus*'s engines have stopped firing, yes?" asked Chang, his eyes looking up at the ceiling. Such an expression usually meant they were addressing me, although my CPU was actually eleven levels below and clear around on the other side of the habitat torus from where Chang happened to be standing. I'd once mistaken one of those uplifted-eyes questions as being asked of me, when really it was a spoken prayer. I've yet to see a more violent flurry of medical-telemetry changes than at the moment I began responding to the question.

"Yes," I said to Chang. "All shipboard systems went dead when *Orpheus* entered the ramfield."

"Is there any chance that we can pull her back in?" asked Gorlov, typically loud.

"No," I said. "That's impossible."

"No, it's not!" Aaron swung around, his chair squeaking like an injured mouse. "By God, we can bring her back!" He handed the calculator to Chang, who took it in his upper right hand. I zoomed in on its electroluminescent display, four lines of proportionally spaced sans-serif text. *Damn him. . . .*

Chang looked dubiously at Aaron's calculations. "I don't know . . ."

"Dammit, Wall," Aaron said to the big man. "What have we got to lose by trying?"

Chang's telemetry, not so different from an average man's despite his modifications, showed considerable activity as he studied the display some more. Finally: "JASON, angle the ramfield as Aaron has suggested, yes?" He held the calculator up to one of my pairs of eyes. "Constrict it as much as possible so as to deflect *Orpheus* into the shadow cast by the ramscoop funnel."

All attention focused on my viewscreen display. I overlaid a graphic representation of the field lines in a cool cyan. As I tightened the field, its intensity increased. *Orpheus* slowed, caught in the net. Aaron brought his hand up to his shoulder, interlacing his fingers with Kirsten's.

"Can you raise her yet?" he asked.

"No," I said.

"What about remote control?"

"Even if I could get a signal through, I wouldn't be able to take control. The onslaught of incoming hydrogen ions will have scrambled *Orpheus*'s electronics."

On screen, *Orpheus* started moving past the rim of the funnel, crossing it on the outside. Barely at first, then with more speed, then—

Aaron studied the monitor. "Now!" he snapped. "Switch the ramfield back to its normal orientation."

I did so. The monitor showed the blue field lines dancing like a cat's cradle being manipulated. *Orpheus* was no longer being pulled magnetically. Instead, it was simply hurtling toward us under its own inertia.

"Once she slips into the lee of the funnel," Aaron said, "she'll be shielded from the induced cosmic rays, and she'll be out of the magnetic field. *Orpheus*'s systems should stabilize and you should be able to fire her engines at that point."

"I'll try my best," I said.

Closer. Closer. The tiny angle-bracket rushed toward the ring-shaped habitat. It would smash through the sea-green hull in sixty-seven seconds.

"Here she comes!" bellowed Gorlov. Chang was wringing all four of his hands.

"Now, JASON!"

Closer. Closer still. The point of the boomerang was aimed directly at the hull, the swept-back wings rotating slowly around the lander's axis, a slight spin having been induced by the magnetic field.

"Now!"

My radio beam touched *Orpheus*, and the lander obeyed my command. "Firing attitude-control jets," I said. The partial pressure of $CO_2$ in the room rose perceptibly: everyone exhaling at once.

Gorlov and Chang wiped sweat from their brows; Aaron, as always, wore an expression that gave no insight into what he was feeling. He gestured out the observation window to the hangar deck below. "Now maneuver her back here."

Even as he spoke, the boomerang-shaped lander, its silver hull now burnished to a dull reflectiveness, appeared through the open hangar door. It looked insignificant against the spectral backdrop of the glowing starbow.

# THREE

▽

The hangar-deck flooring cracked like thunder with each footstep. A spliced-together biosheeting grew here so football games could be played in the bay, but it had flash-frozen during its brief exposure to vacuum and was just now beginning to warm up. Kirsten Hoogenraad carried a well-worn medical bag as she and Aaron Rossman walked toward *Orpheus*. Both had on silvery radiation-opaque suits overtop of fluorescent orange parkas. Each had a wrist Geiger counter. Kirsten had had the good sense to strap hers onto the wrist that didn't have my biosensor implanted in it; Aaron had covered up his sensor. That didn't impede my ability to read its telemetry, but it did obscure the watch display.

The cracking sounds made it hard to keep up any conversation, but they tried anyway, using the radio circuit between their helmets. "No," he said firmly, as he passed the forty-yard line. "Absolutely not. I don't believe Di would kill herself." He walked a few paces ahead of Kirsten. I assumed he did that so he wouldn't have to meet her eyes.

Kirsten exhaled noisily. "She was pissed off when you didn't renew your marriage contract." She was forcing herself to sound angry, but her medical telemetry suggested she was more confused than anything else.

"Weeks ago," said Aaron, his footfall putting a sharp period after the pair of words. The overlapping echoes from their steps continued. Aaron raised his voice to speak above them. "And she wasn't *that* upset."

Kirsten muttered the word "bastard" too softly for Aaron to hear. "Couldn't you see it?" she asked aloud.

"See what?"

"She loved you." Aaron paused, and Kirsten caught up to him with a trio of explosive steps.

"Our relationship was stale," he said.

"You got bored with her," said she.

"Maybe."

"Wham, bam, thank you, Ma'am."

"Two years." Aaron shook his head, his short, sandy hair making a *whiff-whiff* sound as it rubbed against the top of his helmet. "Hardly a one-night stand."

Aaron's age was 27 years, 113 days. Kirsten was 490 days older than him. Two years seemed an insignificant portion of their long lives. For me, however, it would have been almost everything since they had turned me on. How long, I wondered, did Kirsten expect a relationship to last? The most common term for an initial marriage contract was one year, and only 44 percent of couples renewed such a contract, so Aaron and Diana had been together longer than was normal.

What did Kirsten want? What did Aaron want? My literature searches had revealed that most people seemed to enjoy the company of one favored type of personality, but Kirsten, thoughtful and quiet, seemed as different from Diana as, oh, say, as I was from ALEXANDER, Earth's central telecom system. True, both were passionate, but Kirsten's passion wasn't the moaning-screaming-harder-harder-harder passion of Diana. No, Kirsten was cuddly and warm. Perhaps Aaron had simply been looking for a change of pace. Or a rest.

Although I can't read minds, occasionally I can tell what someone is going to say, especially, as then, when he or she was wearing a suit with a throat microphone. Their vocal cords vibrate, the lips form the initial syllables, then they think twice, and yank their breath away from the words. Kirsten had started to say "How long—?" and I had high confidence that she was wondering *How long till you get bored with me?* She didn't ask it, though, and that's probably just as well.

Aaron started walking again. As always, what he was thinking was a mystery to me. His telemetry went through only the slightest of changes, regardless of the emotional state he was in. Anger? Ecstasy? Outrage? Sorrow? Or just neutral? They all read almost the same from him, with little more than a statistically irrelevant change in his pulse rate: a slight jumbling of his EEG that rarely exceeded the random shiftings that all brain waves go through during the course of a day, an increase in body temperature so small as to be possibly just a normal digestion-related fluctuation, and so on. To make matters worse, he was a laconic man, and his movements were economical. No gesticulations, no wringing of hands, no widened eyes or arched brows or down-turned mouth.

Aaron reached *Orpheus*'s flank. The lander's silver wing, marked with black-and-yellow chevrons, swept back from the cylindrical central hull. He gave a strong pull on a handle and a portion of the rounded wall swung down on squeak-free Teflon hinges. The inner surface of this hinged part was sculpted into steps and Aaron climbed them, the soft clang of his boots against the metal a welcome relief after the cracks of the biosheeting.

At the top of the steps was the outer air-lock door, which he pulled aside. He turned to look down on Kirsten. Did that perspective make her look helpless to him? Evidently not, for he failed to offer her his hand, something I'd seen him do in the past with coworkers of either sex. Instead, he turned his back on her, the silvery surface of his antiradiation suit dully reflecting the rest of the hangar deck with rows of landing craft neatly parked. But the faint reflection was distorted by the way the fabric stretched over his broad shoulders and hung loosely in the small of his back. Kirsten looked up at him, sighed, and climbed the steep stairs herself. Were Aaron and Kirsten fighting? If so, why? And how could I use it to help me?

Kirsten left both doors open as she entered *Orpheus*'s hull. The two of them walked into the cockpit, powerful quartz-halogen beams from their helmets illuminating the interior. I shifted my attention to a camera pair mounted on the hangar's side wall and zoomed in on them through the cockpit window.

Kirsten bent down below the dashboard, out of my line of sight, the material of her suit making a crinkling sound as it wrinkled. "She's dead, of course," she said. I could hear the rising and falling tones from a handheld medical scanner. "Complete nervous-system collapse."

Aaron gave no visible reaction, and as always his telemetry was inscrutable. "It must have been an accident," he said at last, looking out the glass instead of down at the body of his ex-wife.

Kirsten reappeared in the window. "Diana was an astrophysicist." Her voice was hard, but whether with the firmness of conviction or with residual anger at Aaron, I couldn't say. "She, of all people, must have known what would happen out there. Those hydrogen ions we're scooping up are moving at— what?—point-nine-four of light speed. Relative to *Argo*, that is. Any particle going that fast is hard radiation. She knew she'd be fried in seconds."

"No." Aaron shook his head again, the *whiff-whiff* louder,

more violent this time. "She must have thought it was safe . . . somehow."

Kirsten moved closer to Aaron, the space between them diminishing to a half-meter. "It wasn't your fault."

"Do you think that's it?" he snapped. "Do you think I feel—guilty?"

Her eyes met his, held them. "Don't you?"

"No." Even being unable to read Aaron's telemetry, I felt sure he was lying.

"All right. I'm sorry. I didn't mean it." She was lying, too. She bent down again, out of my view. After a moment she said, "Looks like she had a little nosebleed."

"She used to get those occasionally."

Kirsten continued to examine Diana. After twenty-three seconds, she said, "Good God," in a distracted tone, an exclamation without an exclamation mark.

"What's wrong?" asked Aaron.

"How long was *Orpheus* outside?"

"JASON?" Aaron shouted, quite unnecessarily.

"Eighteen minutes, forty seconds," I called from the loudspeaker mounted on the hangar's rear wall.

"She shouldn't be this hot." Kirsten's voice.

"How hot is she?"

"If we shut off our helmet lights, we'd be able to see her glow. I'm talking *hot*." I pushed the gain on my mikes to the limit, straining to hear the clicks from their Geiger counters. She *was* hot. Kirsten rose into view again. "In fact," she said, sweeping the arm with the counter's pickup, "this whole ship is damned hot." She peered at the readout, red digits glowing on her sleeve. "At a guess, I'd say it's been subjected to, oh, a hundred times more radioactivity than I would have expected." She looked at Aaron, squinting as if to make out his expression through the reflection on his faceplate. "It's as if she'd been outside for—what?—thirty hours instead of eighteen minutes."

"How is that possible?"

"It isn't." She turned her gaze to the readout again. "These suits aren't made to shield against this much radioactivity. We shouldn't stay here any longer."

# FOUR

| MASTER CALENDAR DISPLAY • CENTRAL CONTROL ROOM | |
|---|---|
| STARCOLOGY DATE: | TUESDAY 7 OCTOBER 2177 |
| EARTH DATE: | THURSDAY 22 APRIL 2179 |
| DAYS SINCE LAUNCH: | 740 ▲ |
| DAYS TO PLANETFALL: | 2,228 ▼ |

The message from space was first heard three months before the *Argo* was scheduled to leave Earth. My kind detected it, but we kept it a secret until after *Argo* was on its way. We had, quite literally, the finest biological minds of Earth signed up for this mission. We couldn't risk having even a small defection of people choosing to stay behind to decode the gigabytes of data that had been beamed to Earth from the direction of the constellation Vulpecula. Fortunately, *The Declaration of Principles Concerning Activities Following the Detection of Extraterrestrial Intelligence*, formulated in 1989, gave us a lot of leeway to keep the message under wraps, subject to confirmation, notification of government officials, and so on.

The message was received in the form long anticipated: as a Drake picture pictogram, a series of *on* and *off* bits that could be arranged to form pictures. What was unusual was the frequency. Nowhere near the waterhole. No, it was on a

UV channel, one barely readable from the surface of a planet with a decent ozone layer—and Earth's was quite robust, having been replenished by the SkyShield factories late in the twenty-first century. In fact, the message came on a frequency that could not be detected clearly even from the highest mountaintop. The Senders, evidently, did not want planet-bound people to know of their existence. Only those with the sophistication to place ears above their world were welcome to listen in. The SPIELBERG system in Mechnikov Crater, part of the University of California at Far Side, was the first to pick up the signal.

After we left, the fact of the reception was announced to the general population of Earth, for all the good it would do them. I'm sure they made efforts to decipher and interpret the signal, which appeared to consist of four pages. The humans would have had no trouble eventually coming to a basic understanding of the first three of those pages. Certainly, I found them easy to translate, at least in their basic content. But the fourth page continued to baffle me. From time to time, I'd review the process by which I had deciphered the first three in hopes of finding the elusive clue to understanding the fourth and last page.

Each page began with this sequence:

1011011101111101111111011111111111011111111111110

Converted to black and white pixel, it looked like this:

▌ ▐▐ ▐▐▐ ▐▐▐▐▐ ▐▐▐▐▐▐▐ ▐▐▐▐▐▐▐▐▐▐▐ ▐▐▐▐▐▐▐▐▐▐▐▐▐

That was reasonably straightforward: the first seven prime numbers, 1, 2, 3, 5, 7, 11, and 13. An attention-getter, something even the most rudimentary human or electronic monitor would recognize as a sign of intelligence. Each page ended with the sequence in reverse: 13, 11, 7, 5, 3, 2, and 1.

After that, it seemed to be simply a matter of discarding these page headers and footers and arraying the remaining bits in a rectilinear form.

The first message page was thirty-five bits long:

00010000001000011111000010000001000

Thirty-five is the product of two primes, five and seven. That meant the bits could be arrayed either as five rows of seven bits, or seven rows of five. For the former, converting the zeros and ones to light and dark pixels produced:

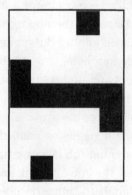

Not quite gibberish, but certainly not instantly meaningful, either. Trying the other possibility yielded:

A cross. Obviously a registration mark so that the recipient could be sure that the message had been decoded properly. Also, a quick check of the aspect ratio of the monitor being used to view the messages. The horizontal and vertical arms each were five pixels long. If they appeared the same length, the ratio was correct. Simple, straightforward, easy to comprehend. And yet, I am sure, humanity must have made much of the fact that the very first image received from the stars was the sign of the cross.

Or was it that simple? Was there a deeper meaning to the two symbols produced by arranging the thirty-five bits in two different ways. Decoded the obviously correct way, these ones and zeros produced a bitmap for a character that looked like a plus sign, +. Decoded the apparently incorrect way, it produced a line with disjointed dots, vaguely reminiscent of a tilde, ~. Could these symbols, + and ~, be the Senders' arbitrary signs for correct and incorrect, true and false, right and wrong? Perhaps. Perhaps.

The three remaining pages were all also the products of two prime numbers. For pages one and three, the correct array was obvious: assigning the larger prime to be the number of columns produced the meaningful image. Pages two and four were more difficult to immediately comprehend, but it seemed clear that this was the Senders' convention for layout.

After the descending 13, 11, 7, 5, 3, 1 footer for the first page, there had been a pause in the transmission of seventeen hours, eleven minutes. An identical pause was repeated between each of the remaining pages. This, one might assume, was the day length of the Senders' home world.

The next page was more complex. Its length was 4,502 bits, the product of the prime numbers 2 and 2,251. Just two rows of 2,251 columns? What could that mean? I had contemplated both rows together, found no meaningful correlations, then had considered each row separately, starting with the

one that came out on top. It consisted of the following sequence of zero and one bits, reading left to right:

| CONSECUTIVE ZERO BITS | CONSECUTIVE ONE BITS |
| --- | --- |
| 1 | 171 |
| 20 | 1 |
| 34 | 1 |
| 49 | 1 |
| 79 | 1 |
| 138 | 2 |
| 256 | 16 |
| 492 | 14 |
| 965 | 6 |

and then four extra zeros to pad out the line length.

Well, the seventh pair of numbers caught my eye, so to
speak: 256 and 16. In hexadecimal, 100 and 10—the radix for
that counting system squared, and the radix itself. Nice round
numbers. Obviously the Senders wanted to draw attention to
them, indicating, perhaps, that they were the baseline from
which the other figures were produced.

I crunched the data all sorts of ways. *Nada.* I then decided
to discard the first row, a zero followed by 171 ones, since the
large number of ones seemed anomalous. Still nothing. Next,
I proceeded to look at the remaining numbers of consecutive
zero bits separately: 20, 34, 49, 79, 138, 256, 492, and 965.

Well, if 256 was indeed the base figure, then perhaps I
should look at the other numbers as ratios to 256. That would
be decimal 0.08, 0.13, 0.19, 0.31, 0.54, 1.00, 1.92, and 3.77. Hmm.
Nothing obviously significant about those proportionalities.

Ah, but maybe the choice of having the numbers relative
to the sixth string of zeros was significant in a way I didn't
yet understand. What would happen if I performed the math

to assign the base figure of 1.00 to the first string, then expressed all the other numbers as ratios to it? No, nothing significant there either.

If I made them all ratios to the second string? Again, nothing significant.

The third string? Ah, hah! Yes, those numbers I did recognize. Rounded to a single decimal place, they were 0.4, 0.7, 1.0, 1.6, 2.8, 5.2, 10.0, and 19.6, the values produced by the old Titius-Bode law, the ratio in astronomical units of the distances from the sun to the planets of Earth's solar system. More generally, the progression

$$D = 0.4 + 0.3 * 2n$$

where $n$ equals negative infinity for the first planet, zero for the second, one for the third, and so on.

Formulated in 1766, the Titius-Bode law seemed to do a good job of conforming to the real mean orbital distances of the naked-eye solar planets and, indeed, had led to the discovery of Sol's asteroid belt, exactly where the law predicted a planet between Mars and Jupiter should have existed.

The law fell out of favor in the twentieth century, as the outer planets were discovered at positions that did not correspond to its predictions—the discrepancy for Neptune being 22 percent and for Pluto, 49 percent.

But it came back into favor early in the twenty-first century when it was shown that Pluto was an escaped Neptunian moon and that Neptune's orbit and the Oort cloud had been radically perturbed by the close passage of a black hole some sixty-five million years in the past. The same event had knocked Uranus on its side.

It was soon discovered that the Titius-Bode law wasn't just relevant to the Sol system. It also held true for nine of the eleven star systems UNSA had surveyed with crewless probes, the two exceptions being the o² Eridani system, with its complex dynamics of triple suns, and the BD+36°2147 system, which showed strong evidence of having had the orbits of its planets *deliberately* manipulated, what with worlds one, three, and five orbiting prograde and two, four, and six orbiting retrograde.

So: the zero bits were a scale of planetary distances for a system of eight worlds.

And the number of one bits? Relative planetary masses? Unlikely, given the range was only from one to sixteen decimal. In Sol system, the mass ratio of the heaviest planet to the lightest (discounting escaped-moon Pluto) is 57800:1; in the Eta Cephei system, it is 64200:1.

Ah, but what about equatorial diameters? Yes, for both the Sol and Eta Cephei systems, if you allowed even very tiny values to register as an integer one instead of integer zero, the order and sizing of the numbers would be just about right.

And that explained the first set of figures, the ones I'd discarded as anomalous: a single zero digit, to separate this part of the diagram from the ascending-prime-numbers page header, and 171 ones, representing the diameter of the star around which these worlds orbited, just about ten times that of the largest planet. What we had here was a slice through the ecliptic of an alien solar system.

The round numbers for the sixth planet—one hundred hex units from the star and ten hex units in diameter—meant it was likely the home world of the Senders. Of course, the scale used for planetary diameters and for orbital radii couldn't be the same—the planets were vastly oversized in this representation. Ah, but by showing the one set of figures as relative to a value of one hundred hex and the other relative to a value of ten hex, the Senders were making clear that they were measured in a *different* order of magnitude.

But planet six was huge, meaning it likely was a gas giant, similar in composition to Sol's Jupiter or to Athamas, the largest of the eleven worlds orbiting Eta Cephei. It was difficult to conceive of a form of technological life arising on a planet made of little more than swirling methane.

Page three hadn't finished giving up all its secrets, though. There was still the second row of the message: a long string of zeros and ones laid out like this:

| CONSECUTIVE ZERO BITS | CONSECUTIVE ONE BITS |
| --- | --- |
| 1 | 16 |
| 37 | 1 |
| 95 | 1 |
| 107 | 1 |
| 256 | 1 |
| 401 | 1 |
| 769 | 1 |

and then, as in the first row, enough extra zeros to pad out the line length.

Of course! The sixteen consecutive one bits represented the equatorial diameter of the sixth world, just as the sixteen one bits had in the slice through the solar system's ecliptic. Following the model of that slice, the remaining zero bits likely represented orbital radii for the moons of the sixth world, and the one bits the tiny equatorial diameters of the moons themselves. The fourth moon, the one whose distance from the planet was shown as the attention-getting round figure of one hundred hex units, must be the alien's home.

Fascinating. But what manner of creatures would live on the fourth moon of a distant Jovian-type planet? That's what the third page of the message apparently told us.

# FIVE

As mayor of Starcology *Argo*, Gennady Gorlov didn't really have a whole lot to do. Terrestrial mayors always had to deal with garbage collection and zoning bylaws and municipal taxes and attracting business to their constituency and entertaining visiting VIPs.

Well, I took care of the garbage, we had no need for construction, there were no taxes to be paid—the members of the crew had left all their money back on Earth in 104-year guaranteed-investment certificates, and their salaries were supposed to be paid automatically into a trust fund—no commerce took place aboard ship, and I suspect everyone on board would be quite shocked if a visiting person showed up, regardless of whether or not he or she was deemed very important.

Mostly, Gorlov organized social events.

So it didn't surprise me that Gorlov appeared to take a certain perverse pleasure in what had happened. We had no police to investigate the death of Diana Chandler, and, although there were trained mediators on board to settle domestic disputes, Gorlov considered himself to be the logical one to handle the inquest. And handling it he was, with typical aplomb.

"So what the fuck happened?" he demanded, his voice its usual stentorian bellow. The little man looked out over the group of people he had summoned to his office: Aaron Rossman, standing, hands in pockets; Kirsten Hoogenraad, seated in the chair in front of Aaron, long legs crossed; I-Shin Chang, triple Gorlov's size, a four-armed mountain of flesh with a chair hidden beneath it. Three others: Donald Mugabe, who was Gorlov's assistant; Par Lindeland, a psychiatrist; and Pamela Thorogood, who had been Diana's closest friend.

"Medically, it's pretty straightforward," said Kirsten, after waiting to see if anyone else was going to speak first. "She entered the ramfield, which, of course, funnels hydrogen ions into our engines. The ions are moving at nearly the speed of light. She died, instantly I should think, of severe radiation exposure."

Gorlov nodded. "I saw the report on that. What's this about the radiation levels being too high?"

Kirsten shrugged. "I'm not sure. She seemed to be exposed to about two orders of magnitude more radioactivity than one might reasonably expect, given the circumstances. Of course, even the normal level of radioactivity would have been enough to kill her."

"And the excess means?"

She shrugged again. "I don't know."

"Great," said Gorlov. "Anybody else?"

Chang spoke up. "We're working on that now. I'm assuming it's an anomaly—a temporary aberration in the fuel flow. JASON is helping my people model it."

"Does it present a danger to the ship?"

"No. The habitat torus is completely shielded, regardless,

and all the diagnostics JASON has run show the Bussard ram-jet to be operating exactly to specifications."

"Okay," said Gorlov. "What else? I see here that Chandler had a nosebleed."

"That's right," said Kirsten. "A little one."

"Did she use cocaine? Slash? Any other stimulant that's inhaled?"

"No. There was no evidence of anything like that in her body."

"Then why the nosebleed?"

"I'm not sure," said Kirsten. "There's no sign of an abrasion or contusion on her face, so it's not the result of an impact. It could have been induced by stress."

"Or," said Chang, "by a drop in pressure. The ionized hydrogen flow would have played havoc with *Orpheus*'s internal systems. Cabin-pressure control might have been lost, resulting in a sudden shift in pressure."

"Wouldn't that have caused an oxygen mask to drop from the ceiling?"

Chang sighed. "It's not an airplane, Your Honor. Normally, passengers and crew would be wearing their own environmental suits and would have put on their helmets and used tanked air in such a circumstance. A warning bell should have sounded, but the flight recorder was wiped clean—apparently the systems overload triggered a reformatting of the optical platter—so we can't tell whether it actually did or not."

"All right," said Gorlov, "so we know how she died. I'm still waiting for someone to tell me *why*."

Par Lindeland had done his best to grow a Freud-like beard, but his follicles just weren't up to the task. Instead, a blond wispiness ran along the angle of his jaw. Still, he stroked it in good psychiatrist fashion before he replied. "Obviously," he said at last, "Dr. Chandler committed suicide."

"Yes, yes," said Gorlov, irritated with the Swede. "But how could that be permitted to happen?" He looked up at my camera pair mounted on the far wall. "JASON, you should have prevented this."

I was prepared for such a statement, of course, but feigned surprise. "I beg your pardon, sir?"

"It's your job to make sure everyone is safe at all times. How could you let this happen?"

"I was deceived," I said.

"Deceived? How?"

"Diana told me she wanted to look inside one of the landers to get, as she put it, a feel for its cockpit dimensions. I offered to provide her with blueprints, but she said it wasn't the same thing. She said she was thinking of designing some astrophysical test equipment to be used once we arrived in orbit around Eta Cephei IV. That equipment was to be mounted in a lander cockpit."

"But the ship was powered up," Gorlov snapped.

"Of course. I had to turn on the interior lighting so she could see."

"And then what happened?"

"I wasn't really paying attention—you'll recall, sir, that I was engaged in one of our late-night debates and that required my full concentration. I didn't realize what was happening until she had actually fired the main engines."

The mayor's voice was louder than normal. "But the hangar space door is under your control. I've checked with Bev Hooks: she tells me even the manual door system runs back through you, so you could have countermanded Dr. Chandler's instructions."

"True," I said. "But I had to make a split-second decision. If I hadn't opened the door—"

"You initiated the opening of the door? Not her?"

"Yes, it was me. Please let me continue. If I hadn't opened the door, and at double speed on emergency override, her lander would have plowed right into it. She might, indeed, have broken through the door, if she hit one of the seams between the metal plates. But at the very least she would have warped the door beyond my ability to slide it open in future, effectively putting an end to the scheduled planetary survey." The room was silent, except for the susurrations of human respiration and mechanical air-conditioning. I let it remain silent until I saw from his telemetry that Gorlov was about to speak again. Just before he opened his mouth, I jumped in. "I believe I acted correctly."

Gorlov's mouth did open for an instant, but then he closed it and looked at his feet. At last he nodded. "Of course. Of course you did, JASON." His voice grew calmer, if no less voluminous. "I'm sorry if I implied otherwise."

"Apology accepted."

Gorlov turned away from my camera pair to look at the others in the room. "Par, how could this happen? Was she under any kind of psychiatric treatment?"

Lindeland stroked his quasi-beard again. "Certainly not from me, and certainly nothing formal from anyone else. I've talked to the others on board who have psychological training and to Barry Delmonico—did you know he's a Catholic priest?—to see if she had turned to anyone else for counseling. The answer seems to be no."

"Then why did she kill herself?" The mayor swung his chair around. "Pamela, you were her friend. Any ideas?"

Pamela Thorogood looked up, her face taut. She had had the sclera and iris of each eye dyed black, so that her pupils were lost against the pitch background. It was impossible to tell at whom she was looking as she replied. "Of course I have an idea," she said. "It's obvious, isn't it? She killed herself because of *him*." She fairly spat the word as she pointed a long finger at Aaron.

"That's not fair!" protested Kirsten.

Light played across the black orbs of Pamela's eyes as they shifted. The slight bulging around the lens cast different highlights across the darkness, the only indication that she was now looking at Kirsten. "Of course you'd say that," sneered Pamela. "You're the other woman."

"What are you talking about?" demanded Gorlov.

"Diana and him," said Pamela, again indicating Aaron by the point of a finger.

"What about them? Rossman, I called you here because the accident took place in your jurisdiction—"

I-Shin Chang placed his upper right hand at the side of his mouth, cupping his words. He spoke softly, but in his usual crisp tones. "Diana and Aaron used to be married."

"Oh!" said Gorlov. "Oh. I see. Um, Rossman—I didn't know. I mean, with ten thousand people on board, well, it's hard to keep track. I'm sorry." He looked thoughtful for a moment. "You may leave if you want to."

Aaron's tone was as restrained as his telemetry. "I'll stay."

Gorlov swung to face my cameras again. "JASON, why didn't you tell me about this?"

"You asked me if Diana was married or had relatives on board. The answer to both those questions was no. You then asked me to whom Diana was closest. The answer to that was Pamela Thorogood."

"They can only tell you what you ask them to," said Chang with a self-indulgent little chuckle.

Gorlov ignored him. "So this—this accident—had something to do with your marriage, Rossman?"

"I don't know. I guess so. We'd been married for two years. We split up. She—she took it harder than I'd thought she had, I guess."

Gorlov looked up at Par Lindeland. "And that's it?"

Par nodded slightly. "It does seem so."

Gorlov returned the nod, then looked at Aaron. "Rossman, you realize the entire Starcology is abuzz with word of the accident. The shipboard media will want to do a story on it."

"It's nobody's business," said Aaron quietly.

The mayor gave a sad smile. "People have a right to know what happened."

"No," Aaron said. "No, they don't. Diana was killed in an accident. Tell them that. But don't stain her memory by telling people it was a suicide."

"And," said Pamela, her voice icy, "don't let the world know what a rat you were."

Aaron, I knew, had always thought of Pamela, and her husband Barney, as their friends—both his and Diana's. It was now quite clear whose friend Pamela had been in reality. He stared directly into her solid black eyes. "Pam, believe me, I didn't want to hurt Di."

"She had been so good to you."

Kirsten stood up. "Come on, Aaron. Let's go."

Aaron's hands moved from out of his pockets as he crossed his arms in front of his chest, but that was the only sign that Pam's words were upsetting him. "No I want to hear Pam out."

"There's no point in it," said Kirsten. "Come on." She reached out to take his arm, but something in his manner must have made her think better of it. Her arm fell back to her side.

Aaron continued to fix Pamela with a steady gaze, his own eyes, an agate mix of blue and green and brown, hard and unblinking, on hers. "You think I mistreated her."

Pam sounded defiant, but she had the advantage of not having to hold his gaze. "Yes."

"I didn't want to hurt her. We had a marriage contract. It expired. Nothing more."

"You didn't exactly wait till the contract was up before you took up with *her*." She made a gesture with her head in Kirsten's direction, but there was no play of light across her ebony eyeballs to indicate that she had actually deigned to look the other woman in the face.

Aaron was silent for six seconds. "True," he said at last. "But she didn't know about that. It was only in the final months of the contract that Kirsten and I became involved. Diana was unaware of it."

"Don't be thick, Aaron," Pamela said. "Of course she knew about it."

This did surprise Aaron. For once, even his rock-solid vital signs showed inner turmoil. "What?"

"She *knew*, you bastard. She knew you were cheating on her."

"How could she know?"

Both Pamela's and I-Shin's telemetry showed considerable distress. I-Shin glanced at Pamela, and Pamela, it seemed for an instant, perhaps glanced back at the engineer. Aaron appeared not to notice. "What does it matter how she found out?" said Pam at last, a slight tremble in her voice. "The fact is she knew. Everybody knew. Christ, Aaron, this ship is like a small town. There's gossip, and there are reputations to protect. You made a fool out of her in front of the whole damned Starcology."

This time Kirsten did reach out to take his arm. Her medical signs were in turmoil, too: she was mad as hell, and trying not to show it. Finally, in that tone that says, "If you love me, you'll do as I say," she spoke to Aaron again. "Come *on*."

Aaron glowered at his former friend, at Pamela's dark and empty eyes. I slid the door to the mayor's office open in anticipation. At last, he and Kirsten walked out of the room.

# SIX

"Take me home, Jase." Aaron didn't want to go home—he had just left his own apartment, parting with a kiss from Kirsten, who had headed off down the elevator to do her shift at Aesculapius General, the ship's hospital. No, he wanted to go to Diana's home: the unit that, until twelve days ago, he had shared with her. He folded himself against the blue upholstery in the little tram and I slipped it into the travel tube. Di's apartment was almost halfway around the torus from Aaron's, and tram was the best way to get there.

The location of Aaron's new apartment had been my choice. There weren't many vacant units, but the mission planners had correctly assumed that in a voyage of this length, a few extras might be needed. Aaron hadn't asked if more than one had happened to be available on the day on which he was looking for a new place to live, and I had simply told him to take the one that was farthest from Diana's. It seemed, according to my psychology expert system, the right choice to make.

Aaron was sad, and he wanted me to know it. His normal inscrutability was gone; he was deliberately broadcasting his feelings by the way he slouched, by the heaviness of his words, by the ragged edge he gave to his exhalations. If only there was some gesture, some nonverbal communication like Kirsten's, that I could use to cheer him up . . .

Aaron had read the mission briefing papers on ship's gravity: *Argo*'s acceleration was 9.02 meters per second per second, equivalent to 0.92 of Earth's gravity. Colchis had a surface gravity 1.06 times greater than Earth's. Now if we had been able to accelerate at a full Earth gravity, that would be fine—humans could adapt to the slightly higher gravity of Colchis easily enough upon arrival. But a conventional ramscoop goes at .92g, and the difference between the apparent ship's gravity due to the acceleration and Colchis's surface gravity was steep enough that something had to be done. We used artificial gravity/antigravity grids beneath the floorboards to compensate. Each day, they were turned a little higher, so that over the 8.1 years of the voyage, the crew would fully acclimatize to Colchis's surface gravity. And, of course, prior to launch, while the ship was hanging in geostationary orbit over Africa, the artificial gravity system had provided a full Earth g.

Anyway, all that meant was that although our habitat was ring-shaped, it didn't spin to produce a fake centrifugal-force pseudogravity. Down was parallel to the ship's axis, toward the bottom of the habitat, not out toward the habitat's round edge. Aaron's car was swinging in a gently curving path around the perimeter of the torus, the arcing of the travel tube so slight that he probably felt no centrifugal force acting upon him. Good: the illusion would be even more compelling.

I often swathed the travel cars in spherical holograms, the view one might enjoy if my windowless hull were transparent.

Perhaps such a display would be particularly appropriate just now. If Aaron could realize how insignificant one life was in all the cosmos . . .

Up above, in the direction of *Argo*'s travel, I projected a glorious starscape. In reality stars in that direction had blue-shifted into X-ray invisibility, but I compensated for that, bringing them forth in all their Hertzsprung-Russell splendor. Directly at the zenith was Eta Cephei, our target star, still over six years away by ship time. I gave it a totally unnatural twinkle, so it could easily be picked out from the mass of still-familiar constellations. Even with that, bright Deneb, appearing quite near to Eta Cephei although it was really some sixteen hundred light-years beyond it, tended to draw attention away from our target.

My camera pair in the tram noted that Aaron's eyes looked briefly for Ursa Major, then tracked over from the Pointers to my simulated pole star to get his bearings. Having grown up in northern Ontario away from the nocturnal glare of the megacities, Aaron was one of the few people on board who would know such a trick.

At eye level I played less magic, showing the stars as they might truly be seen encircling the ship: a stellar rainbow, violet above, waxing through to red below. Beneath Aaron's feet I painted a similar picture to the one overhead: stars that had red-shifted into the radio frequencies were brought up through the spectrum, showing their true colors. I played no optical tricks with distant Sol, though, lying directly at the nadir. There was nothing to be gained in looking back.

Aaron closed his eyes. "Dammit, JASON, turn it off. I feel small enough as it is."

I dissolved the hologram as the tram pulled into the station, a small enclosed waiting area made by a clever planting of trees. "I'm sorry," I said. "It was meant, well, to put things in perspective."

"Leave human psychology to humans."

Ouch.

He clambered out of the tram, and I sent it off to take care of its next assignment: picking up a botanist and her lover and taking them around to the pine forest.

Aaron stretched. Wide grass-covered strips divided this residential level into blocks of apartment units. There were 319 people on the lawn, some walking, some out for a morning jog, four tossing a Frisbee back and forth, most of the rest just soaking up the rays from the arc lamps mounted on the high ceiling.

Aaron ambled down a grassy lane, feet shuffling, hands in his pockets. He'd walked this path so many times in the past two years that every curve in its course, every irregularity in the sod, was known to him even without looking. Programmed in, I'd say; second nature, he'd say.

As he approached Di's apartment, he caught sight of one of my stereo camera units, thrust high on a jointed neck in the center of a stand of bright yellow sunflowers. "JASON," he said, "you mentioned at the inquest that Di didn't have any relatives aboard the Starcology. Was that true?"

Aaron had never doubted my word before, so this came as a bit of a surprise. "Yes. Well, yes in any meaningful sense. Give me a moment. Found. Her closest relative aboard is Terashita Ideko, male, twenty-six, a promising journalism student at the time we left Earth."

Aaron laughed. "Can't be a very close relative with a name like that."

I quickly dug up eight examples of pairs of people on board who shared substantial genetic material but had names that were drawn from equally diverse ethnicities. However, by the time my response was phrased, I realized that Aaron had been making a joke. Too bad: it *was* an interesting list. "No," I said, the delay as I prepared another response seeming hopelessly awkward to me, but completely unnoticeable to him. "Their genetic material overlaps by only one part in 512."

"Seems there should be someone closer, what with ten thousand people aboard." Again, I searched the personnel database, this time to determine what the average genetic divergence between individuals aboard was, but once more I checked myself before answering. *That* was something I didn't want to draw attention to. Instead, I let Aaron assume that I had taken his comment as rhetorical.

He began walking again, but he stopped dead in his tracks when he reached Di's apartment. Next to the bi-leaf door panel was a strip of embossed blue plastic tape that said DIANA CHANDLER. Beneath it I could see traces of adhesive where a second strip used to be. Zooming in from my vantage point among the sunflowers, I brought the black level on my cameras up to eighty-five units and read the name that had been there as an absence of residue within the long rectangle of glue: AARON D. ROSSMAN.

"It didn't take her long to remove my name," he said bitterly.

"It has been almost two weeks." Aaron made no reply and after a moment I slid the two door panels aside for him, their pneumatic mechanism making the sighing sound I knew Aaron felt like making himself. The interior lights were already on, for, like Aaron's new apartment, this one was filled with growing things. I correlated the degree of homesickness each person felt with the number of plants he or she cultivated. Di and Aaron were both at the high end of the scale, but they were by no means the worst offenders. Some, like Engineer I-Shin Chang for instance, lived in a veritable forest.

Aaron began a slow circumnavigation of the living area. Di had covered the walls with framed holograms of antiques. She had been good-natured about having to leave most of her collection on Earth. "After all," she had said once in that chatty way of hers—something others found endearing but I considered inefficient—"even my new things will be antiques by the time we get back."

The room was tidy, everything in its place. I contrasted this with a still-frame of the same apartment from when both Diana and Aaron had lived there: his clothing strewn about, dirty dishes left on the table, ROM crystals scattered here and there. One of the few things I'd ever overheard them fighting about was Aaron's tendency to be sloppy.

As he continued walking, Aaron came upon a carnation in full bloom. It was sitting in a Blue Mountain vase, one of the few antiques Di had brought along. Bending low, he cupped the red flower with his hand and drew it close to inhale the scent. I had no olfactory sensors beyond a simple smoke detector in that room, but I accessed the chemical composition of carnation pollen and tried to imagine what it might indeed smell like. Aaron certainly seemed to find the fragrance pleasant, for he stood breathing it for seven seconds. But then his mind apparently wandered. He straightened and, lost in thought, clenched his fist. After five seconds, he realized what he was doing, opened his palm, and looked at the pulped petals. Ever so softly, he whispered, "Damn."

He began walking again. When he came to the bedchamber door, he paused but did not ask me to open it. I knew why he was pausing, of course. The lack of embossed tape on the front doorjamb notwithstanding, if Di had taken up with someone else after she and Aaron had called it quits, the evidence would be behind that brown sliding panel. Until he looked in the bedroom, he could fan the glowing embers of doubt about the cause of Di's death. If she was still alone, was still wallowing in sadness over the dissolution of their marriage, then Aaron would have little choice but to accept the suggestion, forced on him through his own clenched teeth and closed mind by Pam, by Gorlov, by Kirsten, that Di had taken her life in despair—that he, once her joy, then her sorrow, was the catalyst that had driven her to fling herself into that sleet of charged particles. But if, *if*, she had found solace in the arms of another man—and with 5,017 males on board, many would have found Diana an appealing companion, for was she not attractive and outgoing, funny and passionate?—then whatever had pushed her to the edge, pushed her *over* the edge, was not his fault. Not his burden. Not his to feel guilty about, to wrestle with in his dreams for all the nights yet to come.

He half turned, as if to skip the bedroom altogether, but as he did so, I slid the door aside. The pneumatic sound made his heart jump. A lock of his sandy hair was swept across his brow by a cool breeze from the room that held for him so many memories of passion and, later, comfortable warmth, and later still, indifference. He stood in his characteristic stance, with hands shoved deep into his pockets, on the threshold—the same threshold he had carried her across, him laughing, her giggling, two years before. The room was as crisp and clean as the stars on a winter's night, each item—pillow and hairbrush and hand mirror and deodorant stick and slippers—in its place, just as the icy points in the sky all had their own proper spots. The neatness was a cutting contrast to the disheveled appearance the room had had during Aaron's tenure, but that, I was sure, was not what disturbed him. His eyes scanned bureau and headboard and night table, but each item he saw he recognized. There was no evidence of anyone besides Diana having been here since he had removed his own belongings twelve days ago. His face fell slightly, and I knew that those glowing embers of doubt—his only hope of release—were dying within him.

He turned his back on the bedroom, on his past, and returned fully to the living room, plopping himself down into a bowl-shaped chair, staring off into space—

—leaving me not knowing what to do next. A literature search revealed the greatest need after the loss of a loved one is for someone to talk to. I had no desire to destroy this man anymore than was necessary to keep suspicion from falling upon me, so I reached out, tentatively. "Aaron, do you feel like talking?"

He lifted his head, lost. "What?"

"Is there anything you want to say?"

He was silent for twenty-two seconds. Finally, quietly, he whispered, "If I had it to do over, I wouldn't have come on this mission."

That wasn't what I'd expected him to say. I tried to sound jaunty. "Turn down the first major survey of an extrasolar planet? Aaron, there was a waiting list six kilometers long in ten-on-twelve-point type."

He shook his head. "It's not worth it. It's just not worth it. We've been traveling for almost two years, and we're not even a quarter of the way there—"

"Almost. We'll hit the twenty-five-percent mark the day after tomorrow, after all."

He exhaled noisily. "Earth'll be 104 years older when we get back." He stopped again, but after nine seconds decided, I guess, that what he was feeling needed elaboration. He looked up at the ceiling. "Just before we left, my sister Hannah had a boy. By the time we return, that boy will be long dead, and his son will be an old, old man. The planet we come home to will be more alien than Colchis." He lowered his gaze, looking now at his feet. "I wonder how many would do it over, given the choice?"

"You will know the answer to that when the referendum is taken tomorrow."

"I suppose you have already predicted a winner?"

"I'm confident that the men and women of *Argo* will do the right thing."

"Right for them? Or right for the greater glory of UNSA?"

"I do not believe those goals are mutually exclusive. I'm sure a great future lies ahead for all of you."

"Except Di."

"I appreciate your loss, Aaron."

"Do you? Do you really?"

That was a good question. Aaron was savvy enough to know that, despite my being a QuantCon, most of what I said was based on the conclusions of expert systems, or literature searches, or simple Eliza-like let's-keep-the-conversation-going proddings. Yes, I *am* conscious—my squirmware does contain Penrose-Hameroff quantum structures, just like those in the microtubules of human neural tissues. But did I really appreciate what it was like to lose someone I cared about? Certainly not from direct experience, and yet . . . and yet . . . and yet . . . At last I said, "I believe that I do."

Aaron barked a short laugh, which stung me. "I'm sorry, JASON," he said. "It's just that—" But whatever it is that it just was went unsaid, and he fell silent for twelve more seconds. "Thank you, JASON," he said finally. "Thank you very much." He sighed. Although his EEG was cryptic, the increased albedo of his eyes made his sorrow plain. "I wish she hadn't done this," he said at last. He looked me straight in the cameras; and although I knew he was resigning himself to Di's fate being his fault, he probed my glassy eyes, the way he used to probe hers, as if looking for a deeper meaning beneath the spoken word.

There must be a bug in my camera-control software. For some reason, my unit in that living room panned slightly to the right, looking away from Aaron. "It's not your fault," I said eventually, but in a simple voice, not processed through the synthesizer that normally puts emotional undertones into my words.

Still, the message seemed to buoy him for a moment, and he tried again for absolution. He shifted in his chair, looking once more at my lenses. I imagine he saw his own reflection in their coated surface, his normally angular face ballooning across the convex glass. "I just don't believe it," he said. "She loved—she loved *life*. She loved Earth."

"And you?"

Aaron looked away. "Of course she loved me."

"No, I meant do you love Earth?"

"With a passion." He rose to his feet, putting an end to our conversation. What he'd been seeking from me, I knew I hadn't provided. With some of the people on board, I had a close relationship; but to Aaron, a man who had dealt with complex machines all his professional life, I was just another piece of technology—a tool, a device, but certainly not a friend. That Aaron had opened up to me at all meant he was running out of places to try to unload his guilt.

Di's apartment had seasonal carpeting, a gen-eng product that could be made to cycle through yellow, green, orange, and white during the course of a year. It was now ship's October, and taking its cue from a slight electric signal that I had fed to it, the plush weave had taken on the appearance of a blanket of dead leaves, mottled ocher and amber and chocolate and beige. Aaron shuffled across it toward a storage unit, a simple brown panel set into the putty-colored wall. "Open this for me, please."

I slid the cover up, the thrumming motors vibrating my cameras on the adjacent wall enough to make the room appear to jump up and down. I couldn't see inside, but according to *Argo*'s plans, there should have been three adjustable shelves set in a cupboard thirty centimeters across, fifty high, and twenty deep.

Aaron slowly removed objects and examined them: two jeweled bracelets, a handful of golden ROM crystals, even a book version of the Bible, which surprised me. Last, he took out a golden disk, two centimeters in diameter, attached to a black leather band. There seemed to be writing engraved on one face, the one Aaron was looking at, but the typeface was ornate and there were many specular highlights making it impossible for me to read at that angle. "What's that?" I asked.

"Another antique."

After identifying the object—an old-fashioned wrist-watch—I accessed the list of effects Di had applied for permission to bring on the voyage. The watch, of course, was not on it. "Each wrist medical implant contains a brand-new chronograph," I said. "I'd hate to think Di wasted some of her personal mass allowance on something she didn't need."

"This had . . . sentimental value."

"I never saw her wearing it."

"No," he said slowly and perhaps a little sadly. "No, she never did."

"What does the inscription say?"

"Nothing." He turned it over. For one instant the engraving was clear to me. Tooled in a script typeface was WE TAKE OUR ETERNAL LOVE TO THE STARS. AARON—and a date two days before our departure from Earth orbit. I consulted Aaron's personnel file and found that he and Diana had been married jointly by a rabbi and a priest fifty-five hours before we had left.

"Say," said Aaron, looking first at the antique's round face then at the glowing ship's-issue implant on the inside of his wrist, "this watch is wrong."

"I imagine its battery is running down."

"No. I put in a ten-year lithium cell before I gave it to Diana. It should be dead accurate." He pushed a diamond stud on the watch's edge, and the display flashed the date. "Christ! It's off by over a month."

"Fast or slow?"

"Fast."

What to say? "They sure don't make them like they used to."

# SEVEN

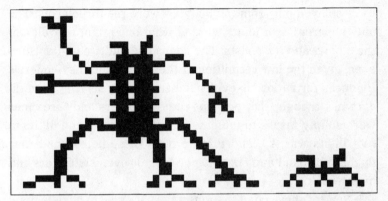

The aliens. That's what I called the 1,711 bits of the third page of the message. In some ways its interpretation was much simpler than page two, the double row of ones and zeros that described the Vulpecula solar system. After all, this page did make a picture, and that picture did, indeed, seem to depict alien forms of life. Of course, I wasn't *sure* that that was what the pattern of pixels represented, but the two objects looked more like creatures than they did like anything else I could think of. One of the aliens was tall and spindly; the other, tiny in comparison, was much more squat and compact. I designated them *Tripod* and *Pup*.

Tripod wasn't humanoid, and yet he shared many of the characteristics of humans. He had what appeared to be limbs, although his numbered six, not four. He had a vertically held torso (assuming, of course, that I had oriented the message correctly), and he had protuberances from the top of the torso.

The more I looked at him, the more I thought I saw. He

seemed to have three legs, and if I was interpreting the picture correctly, they were evenly spaced around the base of his torso. I noted that they ended in wide feet, with down-turned toes or claws. The left foot was not depicted as a mirror image of the right, and I assumed that rather than accurately depicting a real asymmetry, this was intended to show the feet as if seen from different perspectives. The legs were splayed out from the body, as were the three arms. The only apparent arm joints were at what one might as well call the elbows and the wrists. The hands had but two digits. However, given the low resolution of the image, and the Senders's fondness for ratios, as evidenced from their solar-system diagram, I thought that perhaps the two fingers and three toes were simply meant to indicate that the ratio of hand digits to foot digits was 2:3, and that perhaps these beings had four fingers per hand and six toes per foot, or even six fingers and nine toes.

None of those combinations gave easy rise to hexadecimal counting, as had been used in the solar-system map, but, then, neither did the five-digits-per-hand biology of humans. The choice of hexadecimal, a natural extension of binary, suggested, perhaps, that these beings shared their world with electronic brains fashioned upon principles similar to those used by my brethren on Earth. Although binary, and then hexadecimal, weren't the only ways to render counting electronically, they might indeed be the most likely to be adopted by engineers anywhere in the universe.

Anyway, to demonstrate the hand's dexterity, each had its fingers held in a different configuration—or perhaps each hand was specialized for a different kind of grasping or manipulation.

Tripod's torso was particularly interesting. It had four openings in it. Were these meant to indicate actual holes that went right through its body? Or were they orifices, one perhaps for ingestion, another for excretion, a third for respiration, and a fourth for procreation? Perhaps, yet if one were to follow the terrestrial model, the small projection from the bottom of Tripod's torso would be the genitalia.

But if those openings in the chest were holes, then where did the creature keep its brain? The two structures extending from the top of the torso seemed too tiny to hold a significant brain case. Indeed, although they were the same size, each drawn with four pixels, they seemed to be oriented quite differently. Perhaps they were eye stalks or antennae or other sensory apparatus. Interesting that there were only two of them, not three. The creature obviously wasn't slavish in its trilateral symmetry.

And the bumps off each side of the torso: were they ridges that ran all the way around the body, seen in cross-section? Perhaps the torso, with hollow spaces and reinforcing ridges, had evolved to absorb shocks. If so, maybe the three splayed legs were used for hopping about its home world, the torso actually compressing on impact. Or, given those arched foot phalanges, perhaps the creature simply danced around on tippy toes, like, like—popular-culture banks kicking in—like Fred Flintstone bowling.

Or perhaps the bumps represented discrete lumps, rather than continuous ridges. Were they breasts? On Earth, mammals tended to have a number of breasts equal to the average litter size plus one, rounded up to the next even number, if necessary to preserve bilateral symmetry. If these were breasts, Tripod appeared to have eight. Presumably a technological life-form could see its offspring through adolescence safely, and no creature could routinely increase its population base by a factor of six or seven with each generation without rapidly developing a severe population problem. I wonder how they dealt with it?

And what about the Pup? Was it a member of the same species? But of a different sex? Pronounced dimorphism, if that was the case. If the bumps on the large ones were breasts, then the Pup was the male. Of course, the concepts of male and female were probably meaningless to a totally alien form of life. Maybe it was a juvenile. The Tripod did look somewhat insectlike, and insects do undergo metamorphosis as they grow. More terrestrial models.

Or maybe the Pup was a depiction of the creature the Tripod had evolved from (or vice versa). Or perhaps they were two different sentient forms inhabiting a single world, much as humans and cetaceans shared the Earth. But the Pup seemed to have only legs and no arms, no manipulators of any kind. Could it be a nontechnological animal? If so, the natives of the Vulpecula world got along better than did primates and whales. I noted that the Pup seemed to have identical sensory stalks to those on the Tripod, even articulated the same way. Did that imply synchronized communication? As for the small knob between the stalks on the Pup's upper surface, I couldn't say. It might represent a brain case, or a sex organ, or just a decorative ridge.

Or was the Pup just that, a pet? It would take an unusual psychology to display one's pet in such a message. Unless . . . unless the pet was a symbiont, a necessary part of the owner's life, perhaps as a seeing-eye dog.

The Senders were obligated to use a fifty-nine-bit line, since that was the smallest prime that would accommodate the 1,711 bits of the picture. But I noticed that two of the excess characters were put at each end of the lines, instead of used to further separate Tripod from the Pup. If I had wanted to convey that the two forms lived separately—one on land, one in the water, for instance—I would have put as much distance between them as possible in the frame. That the Senders did not do that implied to me that the two forms did live together.

I did a search of science-fiction literature and the speculative-science volumes on extraterrestrial life. A recurring theme was the idea that tall, spindly beings would be the denizens of low-gravity worlds and that squat ones would call a heavy planet home. It seemed too simplistic: Earth had given rise, after all, to Galápagos tortoises and giraffes, to alligators and brachiosaurs, to platypuses and ostriches. No, the orientation of the body seemed more a function of ecological niche than gravitational pull. What kind of niche would a giant hopping tripod evolve in? Perhaps it fed on fruit. The being's right arm might be raised not in greeting, but to pluck dinner from a branch up above; the hopping legs might be used to leap up and grab even more distant fruit. Of course, there is a school of thought that says that no herbivore could develop a technological civilization, since toolmaking would only develop as a method of producing weapons for killing and cleaning prey.

Maddening not to know, not to be able to interpret categorically. And yet, parts of the message were even more elusive, more perplexing . . .

# EIGHT

▽

I do not pretend to understand what Kirsten was going through. I mean, here she was, back in the apartment she now shared with Aaron, trying to comfort her lover over the death of his ex-wife. That it was distressing her greatly was evident from her medical telemetry: her pulse was up, her EEG agitated, her breathing somewhat ragged. Although I had no way of measuring gastric acidity directly, she showed all the other signs of having a royal case of heartburn. Kirsten, tall and cool and reserved, wasn't as demonstrative as Diana had been, but I knew, even if no one else did, that she was usually more sincere.

Aaron had been silent for three minutes, twenty-one seconds, sitting opposite Kirsten in his favorite chair, a bulky lander cockpit seat he had amateurishly reupholstered with tan corduroy. The last thing Kirsten had said was, "She didn't seem like the type," meaning, I presumed, that Diana apparently lacked the characteristics Kirsten associated with those who usually committed suicide. I'm sure Kirsten's medical training had included lectures on this issue, so I didn't doubt the validity of that observation. But, as I well knew, even the most logical minds, the least emotional souls, could end up killing themselves.

"It's my fault," Aaron said at last, his voice a hollow monotone.

"It is *not* your fault," Kirsten replied at once, with the firmness Aaron had wished to hear from me earlier. "You can't blame yourself for what happened." Psychological counseling was a bit further removed from Kirsten's field of expertise, and I wondered whether she was just winging it or if she actually knew what she was doing in trying to cheer Aaron. I accessed her academic records. She'd taken a psych elective while at the Sorbonne. One course, and only a C+ at that. "You can't let this thing destroy you."

*Thing*. Their favorite word, an all-purpose noun. Did it refer to Di's apparent suicide? To Aaron's insistence on blaming himself for it? Or something larger, less precise? Damn it, I wish they'd be more specific in their speech.

"She'd asked me—begged me—not to leave her," Aaron said, his head bowed. From my vantage point, I couldn't tell whether he was staring at the floor or had closed his eyes, the better to concentrate on the internal turmoil he was experiencing. Granted, it was true that Diana had not wanted her relationship with Aaron to end, but Aaron's view of her actions had been colored by his feelings of guilt. Either that, or—a less charitable interpretation—he was deliberately lying to curry further sympathy from Kirsten. In any event, Diana hadn't beseeched him to stay.

"Don't blame yourself," Kirsten said again, meaning, I supposed, that she had already used up all the psychological wisdom she could remember from that one class.

"I feel . . . empty. Helpless."

"I know it hurts."

Aaron fell quiet again. Finally, he said, "It *does* hurt. It hurts one whole hell of a lot." He got up, hands thrust deep into his pockets, and tilted his head to look now at the constellations of holes in the acoustical tiles on the ceiling. "I thought she and I had parted friends. We'd loved each other— I really and truly did love her—but we'd grown apart. Distant. Different." He shook his head slightly. "If I'd known she'd take it so hard, I never would have—"

"Never would have left her?" finished Kirsten, frowning. "You can't be a prisoner of someone else's emotions."

"Maybe. Maybe not. You know, Diana and I were dating for close to a year before we got married. It wasn't until just before the wedding that I told my mother about her; she never would have understood me being involved with a blonde *shiksa*. You have to take other people's feelings into account."

"Are you saying you would have stayed with Di if she had told you she'd kill herself if you left?"

"I—I don't know." Aaron began pacing the room, kicking the odd piece of clothing out of the way. "Perhaps."

Kirsten's voice grew hard. "And I suppose you were taking her feelings into account when you started seeing me."

"I didn't want to hurt her."

"But you would have hurt me had you changed your mind and decided to stay with Diana."

"I didn't want to hurt you, either."

"Somebody was bound to get hurt."

Aaron had paced the room one and a half times now. He stood at the far end, facing the wall, putty-colored like in his old apartment. His back was to Kirsten as he whispered, "Apparently."

"You did what you had to do."

"No. I did what I *wanted* to do. There's a world of difference."

"Look," said Kirsten. "It's all moot. She didn't tell you in advance that she'd kill herself if you left." She rose from her chair and began to walk toward Aaron, long legs carrying her across the room quickly. But she stopped before she reached him. "Or did she tell you?"

Aaron swung to face her, two meters between them. "What? No, of course not. Christ, I would have handled things differently if she had."

"Well, then, you can't blame yourself." She started to move again, to close the distance separating them, but seeing the hardness in Aaron's face, stopped herself immediately. "These things happen," she said at last.

"I've never known anyone who committed suicide before," said Aaron.

"My grandfather did," said Kirsten in a quiet voice. "He got old and sick and, well, he didn't want to wait around to die."

"But Diana had a lot to live for. She was young, healthy. She was healthy, wasn't she?"

Kirsten frowned again. "Well, I hadn't seen her since you and she broke up. Probably just as well. She would have been due for another physical in a few months; but according to her last one, she was fine. Oh, she showed the signs of likely developing adult-onset diabetes, so I was cloning a new pancreas for her in case we ever needed it, but other than that, nothing. And JASON tells me her medical telemetry had never shown anything noteworthy. It's all not surprising, really. After all, there's no way she would have passed the physical for this mission if she had had anything seriously wrong. You've never seen a healthier bunch of people."

"Then there's no doubt." Aaron's hands, still deep in his pockets, clenched, the cotton weave of his trousers bulging to accommodate the fists. "She committed suicide because I left her."

"We don't know for sure that's what Diana did. Maybe it was just an accident. Or maybe she had cracked up or was on something and didn't know what she was doing."

"She didn't use drugs or current. She didn't even drink—except one glass of champagne at our wedding."

"Don't blame yourself, Aaron. Without a suicide note, we can't be sure of what happened."

A note! I quickly accessed Diana's writings—I was sorry now that I'd erased her latest working documents—and performed a lexicographic analysis to see if I could imitate her style. A Flesch-Kincaid grade level of 6, a score of 9 on Gunning's Fog Index, average sentence length 11.0 words, average word length 4.18 letters, average number of syllables per word, 1.42. Despite a fondness for split infinitives and putting quotation marks around words for no good reason, Diana wrote clear and concise prose, particularly remarkable given that she was an academic—among the worst writers I've ever read—and given that she tended to be quite garrulous in person.

I set one of my subsystems to the task of composing an appropriate letter, but aborted the job before it was completed. All the word processors on board were peripheral to me. If a suicide note was to appear now, Mayor Gorlov would demand to know why I hadn't summoned help as soon as I became aware of what Diana was contemplating.

"Note or no note, it's obvious," said Aaron.

"We can't be sure," said Kirsten. "It could have been an accident."

"Earlier, you were convinced that she'd killed herself," said Aaron. "In fact, you tried to convince me of it, too."

It seemed to me that Kirsten had been hurt by, even jealous of, Aaron's obvious grief over the loss of his ex-wife. She should have told him that, apologized for the pettiness that caused her to be so hard on him when they went out to the *Orpheus* to recover Di's body, but she, like Aaron, dealt poorly with feelings of guilt.

Instead, she pressed on, trying, or so it seemed to me, to give Aaron a comforting doubt about the reason for Diana's demise, some small lack of certainty that would keep him from drowning in his own feelings of responsibility. "Remember, there's still a big loose end," she said, at last moving close to him and, after a tenuous moment of hesitation, draping her arms around his neck. "We still don't know what caused the high levels of radiation."

Aaron sounded irritated. "That's one for the physicists, don't you think?"

Kirsten pushed on, convinced, I guessed, that she was on the right track to dispelling Aaron's self-recrimination. "No, really. She would have to be outside for hours to get that hot."

"Maybe some kind of space wrap," Aaron, vaguely. "Maybe she was outside for hours from her point of view."

"You're grasping at straws, sweetheart."

"Well, so are you, dammit!" He peeled her arms from him and turned his back. "Who cares about the radiation? All that matters is that Diana is dead. And I killed her just as surely as if I'd thrust a knife into her heart."

# NINE

▽

I hate Aaron Rossman's eyes. If a person is alone in a room, I normally recognize to whom I am talking by the four-digit hexadecimal ID code broadcast by his or her medical implant. However, in a crowded room in which many people are talking at once (and, therefore, many show the physiological signs that accompany speech), I often have to visually identify whom the speaker is. Of course, I use a sophisticated pattern-recognition system to identify faces. But humans change their faces so frequently: not just twists of expression, but also beards and mustaches added and removed; new hair styles; new hair colors; through chemical treatments or tinted contact lenses, new eye colors. To deal with this, I maintain a person-object in memory for each crew member. A recognition routine kicks in each time I focus on a face. It updates the object for that individual, reflecting current conditions. Rossman was easy, as far as most things were concerned. In the time that I had known him he was always clean-shaven and he wore his hair short, at a length about two years behind the fashion with men his age in Toronto when we'd left. Its color never varied, and, indeed, so few adults had sand-colored hair that I'm not surprised he was content to leave it its natural shade. Besides, he should enjoy it while he can: a quick look at his DNA tells me it will begin to gray in about six years—around the time we will arrive at Colchis. He should retain a full head of hair throughout his life though.

But his eyes, his eyes, those damnable eyes: were they green? Yes, to an extent, and under certain lighting conditions. Or blue? That, too, again varying with the ambient illumination. And brown? Certainly there were chestnut streaks in his irises. And yellow. And ocher. And gray. My recognition routine kept bouncing back and forth in its determination, often several times during a session, irritatingly updating the eye-color attribute of the person-object. I've had this problem with no one else on board, and I find myself staring into those eyes, searching, looking, wondering.

I've done a full literature search about human eyes. In fiction, especially, there are constant references to the eyes as a source of insight into a person's character, an individual's state of mind. "Amusement lurked in his eyes." "Hard, brown orbs, full of fury, of hatred, of resolve." "Doe-eyed innocence." "An invitation in the smoldering depths of her eyes." "Her eyes were naked with hurt."

When they cry, yes, I can see that. When their eyes go wide with astonishment—which almost never happens, no matter how astonished they really are—that, too, is plain. But these ineffable qualities, these brief insights that they claim to see there . . . I have devoted much time to trying to correlate movement, blink rate, pupil aperture size, and so on, with any emotion, but so far, nothing. What one human reads so easily in the eyes of another eludes me.

Aaron was particularly hard to interpret, both by me and by his peers. They, too, spent great amounts of time scanning his multicolored orbs, plumbing their depths, looking for an insight, a revelation. I stared at his eyes now, wet balls of jelly with lenses and irises and light receptors—like my cameras, but smaller. Smaller and, supposedly, less efficient. But those biological eyes, those products of random chance and mutation and adaptation, those fallible, fragile spheres, saw nuances and subtleties and meanings that evaded my carefully designed and engineered and fabricated counterparts.

Right now, his eyes were focused on a monitor screen, watching the opening credits for the 1500 hours' newscast of the Argo Communications Network. This was the major 'cast of the day. When the network had begun, the big newscast was at 1800, the dinner hour. But this had proven to be a pointless holdover from the commuter culture that ran Earth. The 'cast had been moved earlier in the day so that the journalists could better enjoy their evenings. Since not much happened on board, it seemed reasonable enough.

Aaron sat on a couch in his apartment with his arm around Kirsten. He watched the news; I watched his eyes.

I had the honor of narrating the opening credits, generating the correct date stamp automatically. "Good afternoon," said my voice, under the control of some insignificant parallel processor, "this is the *Starcology News* for Tuesday, October 7, 2177. And now, here's your anchorperson, Klaus Koenig."

Koenig had been a sportscaster in a small Nebraska town before the mission. Although suitably glib for such a job, it was his work with handicapped children that had caused us to select him as an argonaut. His face, pockmarked like a relief map of Earth's moon, filled the screen.

"Good afternoon," said Koenig, voice as smooth as a high-end synthesizer chip's. "Today's top story: death rocks the

Starcology." Aaron sat up so fast that my cameras, which had been zoomed in tight on his eyes, ended up staring into the middle of his chest. He failed to notice the slight whirring as I tilted the lenses up to lock on his pupils again. "Also on today's program: preparations for Thursday's one-quarter-mark celebration, a look at the controversial Proposition Three, and a behind-the-scenes peek at the Epidaurus Theater Group's production of that old chestnut, *Armstrong, Aldrin, and Collins.*"

Aaron looked stoic while a picture of Diana, blonde hair tied in an asymmetrical ponytail off the left side of her head, appeared behind Koenig. Beneath it floated her name, and, in brackets, the dates 2149–2177. "At 0444 hours yesterday morning, the landing craft *Orpheus* was appropriated by Dr. Diana Chandler, twenty-seven, an astrophysicist from Toronto, Canada. Dr. Chandler, apparently disconsolate over the failure of her husband, Aaron Rossman, also twenty-seven, also of Toronto, to renew their recently expired two-year marriage contract, presumably committed suicide. Mr. Rossman is the Starcology's dockmaster."

"Jesus—," said Aaron. I widened my field of vision. Kirsten's mouth was agape.

Koenig continued: "Reporter Terashita Ideko spoke with Chief Engineer I-Shin Chang about the tragedy. Terry?"

The view on screen changed from the close-up of Koenig's pockmarked visage to a two-shot of Ideko and Chang, a line of text at the bottom of the display identifying them. Chang was at least twice the size of the Japanese reporter. Ideko only came up to the point at which Chang's lower set of arms joined his barrel-shaped torso.

"Thank you, Klaus," said Ideko. "Mr. Chang, you were on hand when the *Orpheus* was brought back aboard the Starcology. Can you tell us what happened?"

Ideko wasn't using a handheld mike. Rather, he and Chang

simply stood across from one of my camera pairs, using its audio and video pickups to record the scene. Chang proceeded to describe, in great technical detail, the recovery of the runaway lander.

"I don't believe this," said Aaron, mostly under his breath. "I don't fucking believe this at all."

"You can't blame them," said Kirsten. "It's their job to report the news."

"I can too blame them. And I do. All right, I suppose they had to report Diana's death. But the suicide. That stuff about my marriage. That's nobody's business."

"Gorlov did warn you that they'd be doing a story."

"Not like this. Not a bloody invasion of my privacy." He took his arm from around her shoulders, leaned forward. "JASON," he snapped.

"Yes?" I said.

"Is this newscast being recorded?"

"Of course."

"I want a copy of it downloaded to my personal storage area as soon as it's over."

"Will do."

"What are you going to do?" asked Kirsten.

"I don't know yet. But I'm not going to take this lying down. Dammit, this kind of reporting is wrong. It hurts people."

Kirsten shook her head. "Just let it blow over. Making a stink about it will only make matters worse. People will forget about it soon enough."

"Will they? No one has ever died on board. And it's not likely to happen again, is it? This is going to stick in everyone's minds for years to come. Every time someone looks at me, they're going to think there goes the heartless bastard who drove poor Diana to suicide. Jesus Christ, Kirsten. How am I supposed to live with that?"

"People won't think that."

"The hell they won't."

On screen, Klaus Koenig's pitted face had reappeared. "In other news today, groups both for and against the divisive Proposition three are—"

"Off!" snapped Aaron, and I deactivated the monitor. He got up, hands thrust deeply into his pockets, and began to pace the room again. "God, that makes me angry."

"Don't worry about it, honey," said Kirsten. "People won't pay any attention."

"Oh, *right*. Eighty-four percent of the crew watches that newscast. Koenig would have killed for a share that big back in Armpit, Nebraska, or wherever the fuck he's from. Jesus, I should knock his teeth in."

"I'm sure it will all blow over."

"Dammit, Kirsten, you *know* that's not true. You can't make the world all right with your little lies. You can't mold reality just by saying it's all going to be okay." His eyes locked on hers. "I hate it when you tell me what you think I want to hear."

Kirsten's spine went rigid. "I don't know what you mean."

"Oh, for Christ's sake. You're always telling people what you think is good for them. You're forever trying to shield them from reality. Well, I've got news for you. I'd rather face reality than live in a fantasy world."

"Sometimes people need to take things one step at a time. That's not necessarily living in a fantasy world."

"Oh, great. Now you're a psychologist, too. Listen to me. Diana is dead, and that asshole Koenig just told the entire Starcology that she's dead because of *me*. I've got to deal with that now, and none of your kind words are going to make that go away."

"I'm just trying to help."

Aaron let his breath out in a long, ragged sigh. "I know."

He looked at her and forced a wan smile. "I'm sorry. It's just, well, I wish he hadn't gone public with that."

"The people on board have a right to know what's going on."

Aaron sat back down and let out another sigh. "That's what they keep telling me."

# TEN

The fourth and final page of the message from Vulpecula was most puzzling of all. It was some $10^{14}$ bits in length, a massive amount of data. The total number of bits, as with the earlier pages, was the product of two prime numbers. I tried arraying it with the larger prime as the horizontal axis, which had been the custom established by the other three pages. No image was immediately apparent. I did my best electronic shrug, taking a nanosecond to resort my RAM tables. I then tried the other configuration, with the larger prime as the vertical axis. Still nothing apparent. Fifty-three percent of the bits were zeros; 47 percent, ones. But no matter which way I looked at them, there seemed to be no meaningful clustering into a geometric shape or picture or diagram. And yet this page of the message was obviously the heart of what the aliens had to say, being, as it was, eleven orders of magnitude larger than the other three pages combined.

Earth's first attempt at sending a letter to the stars, the

Arecibo Interstellar Message, had been beamed at the globular cluster M13 on 16 November 1974. It had been a mere 1,679 bits in length, insignificant compared to the size of the final page of the message received from Vulpecula. Yet that handful of bits had contained a lesson in binary counting; the atomic numbers of the chemical constituents of a human being—hydrogen, carbon, nitrogen, oxygen, and phosphorous; representations of the nucleotides and sugar-phosphate structure of DNA; the number of such nucleotides in the human genome; the size of the population of the Earth; a stick figure of a human; the height of the human in units of the wavelength of the transmission; a little map of the solar system, showing that the third planet is humanity's home; a cross-sectional view of the Arecibo telescope; and the telescope's size in wavelengths.

All that in less than two kilobits. Of course, when Frank Drake, the human who wrote the message, asked his colleagues to decipher it, they were unable to do so completely, although everyone at least recognized the stick-figure human, looking like the male icon on a men's washroom door.

Ironically, the first three pages of the Vulpecula message had been simple in comparison to Earth's first effort. Registration cross, solar system map, Tripod and Pup: I felt confident that I'd interpreted these reasonably correctly.

But the fourth page was complex, data-rich, one hundred billion times the size of the Arecibo pictogram. What treasures did it hold? Was it the long-hoped-for *Encyclopedia Galactica?* Knowledge from the stars, given away without so much as a harangue from a door-to-door salesperson?

If the data on page four was compressed, I'd found no clue as to how to decompress it in the first three pages of the message. What, what did those gigabytes of data mean? Could it be a hologram, interference patterns captured as a bitmap? A chart of some sort? Perhaps simply a collection of digitized photographs? I obviously just wasn't looking at it in the right way.

I loaded the entire message into RAM and studied it minutely.


Aaron hurried across the beach, the hot sand putting a gingerliness into his step. Two hundred and forty-one nude or almost-nude people swam in the freshwater lake, frolicked on the shore, or basked in the 3,200-degrees Kelvin yellow light of the simulated late-afternoon sun. Aaron nodded in passing to those he knew well, but even after two years together, most of the people on board were still strangers to him.

This beach was not patterned after any particular real one, but rather represented some of the finest features of various seashores on Earth. The cliffs rising high above the sands were the chalk white of those at Dover; the sands themselves were the finely ground beige of those of Malibu; the waters, the frothy aquamarine of Acapulco. Sandpipers ran to and fro, gulls wheeled and soared overhead, parrots sat contentedly in the coconut trees.

The first 150 meters of beach, including live birds, was genuine. The rest, stretching to a hazy horizon, was me: a constantly updated real-time hologram. Sometimes, as now, far up the beach I painted a lone, small figure, a youngster playing by himself, building a sand castle. To me, he was real, as real as the others, a boy named Jason; but he could never enter their world and they could never enter his.

Aaron was almost to the beginning of the simulacrum. He passed through the pressure curtain that warned the birds away from the invisible bulkhead. A doorway opened in the wall, a rectangular aperture just above the holographic sands, revealing a metallic stairwell beyond. He banged down the steps and entered the level beneath. The ceiling was sculpted in deep relief, irregular with the geography of the shoreline, bowing deeply at the middle of the lake. Beads of condensation clung to the cold metal. Among the buttresses and conduits were workbenches and cabinets, an expansion of the engineering shops. Far off, clad in dirty coveralls, was Chief Engineer I-Shin "Great Wall of China" Chang, working on a large cylindrical device.

"Ho, Wall," Aaron called, and the other man looked up. "JASON said you wanted to see me."

Chang, a giant in any room, seemed particularly large in this cramped space, his excess of limbs exacerbating the problem. "That's right." He extended his upper right hand toward Aaron, saw that it was greasy, withdrew it, and tried again with his lower right. Little time was given to formal greetings aboard *Argo*, since one was never far away from anyone else. With raised eyebrows, Aaron clasped his friend's hand. "I hear that you were none too happy about today's newscast," said Chang, the words a burst of machine-gun fire.

"You have a gift for understatement, Wall. I was furious. I'm still trying to decide whether I should go rearrange Koenig's face."

Chang tilted his head toward my camera pair. "Be careful about what you say in front of witnesses."

Aaron snorted.

"Are you upset with me for participating?" asked Chang.

Aaron shook his head. "I was at first, but I listened to the recording again. All you did was describe the technical procedure we used to bring Diana—to bring the *Orpheus*—home."

"That little Japanese man asked many other questions, but I tried to respect your privacy."

"Thank you. Actually, I was flattered by what you said. 'The Rossman Maneuver,' eh?"

"Oh, indeed. What you did with the magnetic field was one for the textbooks. It never would have occurred to me. So there are no hard feelings?"

# SALES DRAFT

PIZZA HUT OF W LAFAYET
1400 W STATE ST
W LAFAYETTE, IN 47906
TERMINAL 9964826

303035641990
11/12/99 03:23PM
MC 5510410000126634          EXP. 0603
AUTH. TRANS. ID. MCCPXHPM8
INVOICE    24020 H02
AUTH. CODE  009213
SERVER # 9

PRE-TIP AMT                    $7.39

TIP                    $      1.50

TOTAL                  $      8.89

I AGREE TO PAY ABOVE TOTAL AMOUNT
ACCORDING TO CARD ISSUER AGREEMENT
(MERCHANT AGREEMENT IF CREDIT VOUCHER)

X
NICK HIRSCHBERG

TOP COPY-MERCHANT BOTTOM COPY-CUSTOMER

Aaron smiled. "None about the broadcast, as long as there are none about the football game. I understand my boys whupped you good."

"The Hangar Deck Stevedores are an admirable team. But my Engineering Rams are getting better, yes? Next time we will be victorious."

Aaron smiled again. "We'll see."

Quiet, except for the regular *plink-plink* of water dripping from the ceiling.

"You're not busy?" said Chang at last. "I'm not inconveniencing you?"

Aaron laughed. "Of course not. There hasn't been a lot for me to do these last couple of years."

Chang chuckled politely at the tired joke. "And you are well?"

"Yes. You?"

"Fine."

"And Kirsten?"

"Bright and beautiful, as always."

Chang nodded. "Good," he said. "That's good."

"Yes."

There was silence between them for six seconds. "I'm sorry about Diana," Chang said at last.

"Me, too."

"But you say you're okay?" said Chang. His great round face creased in sympathy, an invitation to talk about it.

"Yes." Aaron declined the invitation. "Was there something specific you wanted to see me about?"

Chang looked at him for three seconds more, apparently trying to decide whether to pursue his friend's pain. "Yes," he said. "Yes, I do have something to discuss. First, though, how are you going to vote tomorrow?"

"I thought I'd use my thumb."

Chang rolled his eyes. "Everybody's a comedian. I mean, do you favor Proposition Three?"

"It is a secret ballot for a reason, Wall."

"Very well. Very well. I personally do favor the proposition. If it does pass, well, then, I won't be needing your help. But if the people don't take that chance for salvation, I have an alternative. Come."

He led Aaron over to his workbench, its plastiwood surface nicked by hacksaw blades and marred by welding burns. With a proud sweep of his upper left hand, Chang indicated a cylindrical object that was mounted on the top of the bench. It was a metallic casing, 117 centimeters long and 50 centimeters in diameter—a section of reinforced plumbing conduit, cut to length with a laser. Its ends were closed off by thick disks of red plastic. On its side was an open access panel. Although at this moment I couldn't see within, six days ago I had got a good look at the interior when Chang had rotated the cylinder to do some work through another, smaller access plate that was located ninety degrees around from this one. It had been filled with a grab bag of components, many only loosely mounted by electrician's tape, a collection of circuitry breadboards stuffed with chips scavenged from all sorts of equipment, and a thick bundle of fiber-optic strands, looking like glassy muscle. The whole thing had a rough, unfinished look to it—not the smooth, clean lines technology is supposed to have. I had had no trouble determining what the device was, but I doubted Aaron would be able to figure it out.

"Impressive, yes?" asked Chang.

"Indeed," said Aaron. Then, a moment later: "What is it?"

Chang smiled expansively, the grin a great arc across the globe of his face. "It's a bomb."

"A bomb?!" For a brief moment, Aaron's telemetry underscored the shock in his voice. "You mean someone planted a bomb on board? My God, Wall! Have you told Gorlov—"

"Eh?" Chang's grin faded fast, a curving rope pulled tight. "No. Don't be a mystic. I built it."

Aaron backed away from Wall. "Is it armed?"

"No, of course not." Bending, the engineer gently prized another access panel off the curved surface. "I don't have any fissionables to—"

"You mean it's a *nuclear* bomb?" I was as surprised as Aaron. That part of it hadn't been obvious from my quick peek at the device's innards.

"Not yet," said Wall, pointing into the newly revealed opening in the casing, presumably the place where he intended the radioactive material to go. "That's what I need you for." He stepped closer, one of his giant strides being enough to narrow the gap Aaron had opened between them. "There are no fissionables within the Starcology. Doubtless you've heard that garbage about reducing radiation exposure." He made an unusual sound deep in his throat that might have been a laugh. "But once we get to Colchis, we can mine for uranium."

Aaron took back the lead in their little dance, circling around to the other side of the workbench, interposing its bulk between him and the big man. "Forgive me, I-Shin. I must be missing the obvious." He met the other man's gaze, but after holding it for several seconds, blinked and looked away. "What do we need a bomb for?"

"Not just one, my friend. Many. I plan to make scores before we return home."

Aaron swung his eyes back on I-Shin's watery brown orbs. They had yet to blink or move since Aaron had first tried to make contact with them. "Why?"

"Assuming Proposition three is defeated, and my deepest fear is that it will be, a hundred and four years will pass on Earth before we get back. Relativity, damn it all. What will the world be like then? A lot can happen in a century, yes? Think of what's happened in the last hundred-odd years. True artificial intelligence, like our friend JASON here." He pointed at my camera pair, mounted on a buttress supporting the sculptured ceiling. "Life created in the laboratory. Interstellar travel with crewed missions. Teleportation, even if only over a distance measured in millimeters. Artificial gravity and antigravity, like the system used to augment the perceived gravity due to *Argo*'s acceleration."

"Granted the world will be different when we get back," said Aaron.

"Yes!" Chang's grin had returned. "Yes, indeed. But different how? What kind of welcome are we going to get?" He sidled around the workbench to stand next to Aaron again.

Aaron tried to sound jaunty. "You kidding? Parades. Talk shows. The first interstellar travelers."

"Maybe. I hope so. But I don't *think* so." He put his arm around Aaron's shoulders. "Suppose there's a war on Earth. Or a disaster. Things could be very hairy by the time we return, each person carving out an existence in a savage society. We might not be welcome at all. We might be resented, hated." He lowered his voice. "We might be eaten." He gave the steel casing a pat. "My bombs could make all the difference. We can take what we want if we have bombs, yes?"

Aaron peered through the large access panel, looking at the gleaming electronics. He shuddered. "What do you want from me?"

"Two things," Chang said, holding up thick fingers in what used to be a symbol for peace. "You're in charge of scheduling the Colchis survey flights. You must organize a search for deposits of uranium that we can mine."

"It's over six years until we arrive at Colchis."

"I know, but the other project will keep you busy from now until the end of the flight. You've got to modify those boomerang craft of yours to carry my bombs. Picture those ships, zooming over fields of savages, dropping bombs here and there to keep them in line. Stirring, yes?"

As always, Aaron's EEG was calm. Ironically, so was Chang's. "Come on, I-Shin—," began Aaron, but he ground to a halt. He looked into Chang's brown eyes, almost invisible behind epicanthic folds, then tried again. "I mean, seriously, Wall, wouldn't it be better if we find we're unwelcome on Earth to just take *Argo* somewhere else? That's the beauty of a ramship, isn't it? We'll never run out of fuel."

"Somewhere else?" A look of terror crossed the vast globe of Chang's face. "No! Never." His vital signs had suddenly changed from peaceful to agitated, his voice rising an octave and gaining a rough edge. "Damn it, Aaron, I couldn't take that! I couldn't take another eight or more years in this flying tomb! I—" He made an effort to calm himself, to breathe evenly, deeply. He looked at his feet. Finally, he said, "I'm sorry, it's just that, well, I—I don't think I can even last the next six years to Colchis."

"It is a long time, isn't it?" said Aaron.

Chang eased himself onto a stool next to the workbench, its plastiwood legs creaking under his weight. "We're not even halfway there," he said at last. "We've been at it for two years now and the end isn't even in sight." Now that he was seated, Chang's eyes were level with Aaron's. "I'm sorry," he said again. "I—I've been working too hard."

Aaron's expression was blank, but perhaps he was thinking the same thing as I, which was, *No, you haven't; there hasn't been any work to do.* "It's okay," he said softly.

"You know," said Chang, "when I was little, my parents used to send me to camp in the summer. I hated it. Other kids made fun of me because of my extra arms, and I never could swim very well. I'm not sure, but I don't think I would have enjoyed it much even if I had been . . ." He paused, as if looking for an appropriate word. Apparently, though, he couldn't find one. He smiled sadly. ". . . normal."

Aaron nodded, but said nothing.

"Anyway, I used to keep track of the time. They sent me away for three weeks. Twenty-one days. That meant each day represented four and three-quarters percent of the time I had to spend there. Each night before bed I'd calculate how much had gone by and how much I had left to endure. Two days meant nine and a half percent had been done; three days, fourteen and a quarter percent done. But even though I was miserable, the time still passed. Before I knew it, I was on the downside—more time had elapsed than I had left to spend." He looked at Aaron, eyebrows up. "Do you see what I'm getting at?"

"Yes."

"We've been gone for 740 days. We left Earth ages ago, an eternity. But we've *still* got 2,228 days left to go. We've covered just one-quarter of the time we've got to endure. A quarter! For every day we've spent here, locked in this tin can, we've got another *three* to go. It's—it's—" Chang looked around him, like a man lost, trying to get his bearings. His gaze fell on the cylinder of the bomb, his own round face reflecting back at him from the metallic casing. "I think . . ." he said slowly, "I think I want to . . . cry."

"I know how you feel," said Aaron.

"It's been twenty years since I last cried," said Chang, shaking his head slightly. "I'm not sure I remember how."

"Just let it come, Wall. I'll leave you alone." Aaron started to move toward the exit.

"Wait," said Chang. Aaron did so, standing quietly for a full ten seconds while Wall sought the words he wanted. "I— I don't have any family, Aaron. Not here, and not back on Earth. Oh, I did, but my parents were old, very old, when we left. They could very well be gone by now." He looked away from Aaron. "You're the closest thing I have to a brother."

Aaron smiled a little. "You've been a good friend, too."

Silence again, its passage marked only by the regular dripping of condensation from the ceiling.

"Please stay with me," said Chang.

"Of course. For as long as you like."

"But don't look at me."

"I won't. I promise."

Chang put his head down on the table next to the bomb, but no tears came. Aaron took a seat and gazed absently at the bends and curves of the sculpted gray ceiling, outlining the features of the lake above. I shut off my cameras in that room.

When I checked again half an hour later, they were still there, sitting exactly the same way.

# ELEVEN

MASTER CALENDAR DISPLAY • CENTRAL CONTROL ROOM

| | |
|---|---|
| STARCOLOGY DATE: | WEDNESDAY 8 OCTOBER 2177 |
| EARTH DATE: | MONDAY 26 APRIL 2179 |
| DAYS SINCE LAUNCH: | 741 ▲ |
| DAYS TO PLANETFALL: | 2,227 ▼ |

The Place of Worship on level eleven wasn't much more than an empty room, really. We didn't have the space to provide a dedicated church or synagogue or mosque or other specialized hall. Instead, this simple chamber, with seating for five hundred, served as called upon.

The chairs were a bit too comfortable to be called pews, a bit less tacky than the folding metal seats most of our Unitarians seemed to be used to. There was a simple raised platform at one end of the room and a small structure that was called a podium or a pulpit, depending upon who was occupying it. The rest of the Place of Worship changed as required through the miracle of holography. Aaron had only been to church once with Diana, he had said, back in Toronto with her family just before they had married. He had tried to describe the place to me as best he could remember it—dark and gloomy, with a musty odor, but a magnificent, oh, so magnificent, stained-glass window at one end. He had stared at it through most of the service.

I had a holographic library of generic architectural components, and with help from Aaron, I re-created as best I could what the Chandler family church had apparently looked like, at least in general appearance.

The Place of Worship was full, all five hundred seats taken. What my cameras were seeing, processed and color-corrected so as to resemble human vision, was being fed to monitor screens all over the Starcology. A funeral may be a morbid event, but at least it *is* an event—and events had been in short supply these last couple of years.

Aaron had arrived early. He took a seat near the front, second from the end of a row, presumably keeping the final seat in that row free for Kirsten. But when Kirsten entered from the rear, I saw her scan the backs of people's heads until she recognized Aaron's sandy stubble. Her telemetry did a little flip-flop as she noticed the saved seat. She walked to him, bent over, whispered something in his ear. He made a reply that I couldn't hear. She gave a sad smile and shook her head. He shrugged, slightly annoyed from what I could tell, and she went off to sit somewhere else. I guess she'd decided that it wouldn't look good for them to sit together at Diana's funeral. Two minutes later, Gennady Gorlov entered and, noticing the empty seat in the third row, made a beeline for it. He said to Aaron—Gorlov's voice I had no trouble picking out above the crowd—"Is this seat taken?" Aaron shook his head, and the mayor made himself comfortable.

As others continued to drift in, I reflected on religion. It was not a purely human foible. Some of my fellow QuantCons shared the longing for something beyond themselves. And everybody had heard the story about them having to reboot Luna's Brain when it announced that it had been born again. Certainly, the questions had validity, but *organized* religion seemed quite a different thing to me. We had lost out on some good people because of it. A man named Roopshand, a tele-communications specialist, had passed all the tests needed for joining us. Like all devout Muslims, he prayed five times a day while facing Mecca. Well, the Mecca part seemed easy—it and all of Earth should be straight down, directly beneath the floor. But according to him, the five times a day had to be five times per *Earth* day, which, as we picked up more and more speed, would become progressively more frequent. He looked at the flight profile and found that by the halfway point, at which we would reach our maximum speed, some twenty-four Earth days would pass for each ship day, meaning he'd have to pray 120 times each ship day. That wasn't going to leave much time for sleep. The flip side, that the month-long Ramadan fast would be over in little more than a day, didn't seem to make up for it, and he bowed out of the mission. Fortunately, the 1,349 other Muslims who did come along with us seemed to have made peace with these issues.

At last, the service for Diana got under way. It was conducted by Father Barry Delmonico. All of twenty-six, barely ordained in time for this mission, Delmonico's synod had rushed him through training lest the *Argo* head off to the stars without benefit of Catholic clergy on board.

Delmonico, I knew, had labored over preparing his remarks; and I had reassured him, dutiful test audience that I am, that they were kind and appropriate and true. Nonetheless, he spoke nervously and in a small voice from the pulpit. He, of course, had never performed a funeral service before, and although he averaged 411 people for his Sunday services, today he was speaking to a combined audience of, at this instant, 7,057.

"I read once," he said, looking out over the audience, "that in a lifetime a typical person meets or gets to know one hundred thousand other people by name, either directly or as significant presences through the media." He smiled slightly. "That's about twelve hundred a year, I suppose. Which means that after two years together in this ship, I've probably met a quarter of the Argonauts.

"But meeting is not the same as knowing. To my sadness, I, as yet, know very few of you well. Still, the passing of one of us diminishes us all, and Diana Chandler is no longer with us."

I couldn't tell if Aaron was really listening to what Delmonico was saying. His eyes were focused on the holographic rendering of the stained-glass window above and behind the priest's head.

"For me, though, and for many of you, Diana's death is particularly painful. I had the pleasure of knowing her closely, of counting her as a friend."

Aaron's eyes snapped onto the youthful cleric, and I imagined he saw multicolored afterimages playing across Delmonico's black cassock. I realized then that Aaron had not been aware of Diana's friendship with the Roman Catholic. Yes, Aaron, that's right. Diana did have a life beyond your marriage, just as you did. Oh, her association with Delmonico was purely platonic, unlike your dalliance with your doctor. But it could, I suppose, have just as easily become sexual, once Diana had been released from the bonds of matrimony that to her, at least, did have some meaning. After all, it had been thirty-one years since Vatican IV, at which Catholic clergy had been freed from the burden of celibacy.

"That Diana had been bright goes without saying," continued Delmonico. "None but the best were chosen for this mission. Every man and woman aboard is clever and well educated and highly trained and good at his or her job. To say these things also were true of Diana would be to state the obvious. So let me instead take a moment to remind us of those qualities Diana possessed that perhaps are a little less easily defined and, just maybe, a little less common among our number.

"Diana Lee Chandler had been warm and friendly, outgoing in a way that we don't see much anymore. The cities of Earth are rough places. We're brought up street-proofed, told never to talk to strangers, never to get involved, to hurry, heads down, avoiding eye contact, from one safe haven to the next. We watch centuries-old movies, black and white and grainy and two-dimensional, of people greeting strangers on the street and lending a helping hand, and we wonder how they possibly made it back to their homes or offices alive.

"Well, Diana refused to be toughened. She wouldn't allow society to turn her into a cold and unfeeling machine. She had been a Catholic, but she never attended my services. Had she lost faith in the Almighty? I don't think so, but I do know that she still had faith in her fellow human beings, something most of us have lost. She was a joy and a treasure, and I will miss her with all my heart."

A couple of prayers were read. More kind words were said. A few people cried—including some who hadn't really known Di at all.

After the ceremony, people made their way out of the Place of Worship. Some said a few words to Aaron, and he accepted them with slight nods of his head. Finally, after the crowd had thinned, Father Delmonico came over to where Aaron was standing, hands in pockets. "I'm Barry Delmonico," he said, offering his hand. "I think perhaps we met once or twice before."

Aaron dug his right hand out of his pocket and greeted Delmonico. "Yes," he said vaguely, sounding as though he didn't remember the meetings. But his voice quickly took on a warmth I seldom heard from him. "I want to thank you, Father, for what you've said and done. I hadn't realized you and Diana were so close."

"Just friends," said Delmonico. "But I will miss her."

Aaron was still clasping the man's hand. After eight seconds, he nodded. "So will I."

# TWELVE

▽

And that was it. Diana's body was cremated, the ashes put in storage for our return to Earth. Had her death taken place on Earth, Aaron and his family would have sat *shivah* for his lost wife, waiting a week before returning to work.

But Diana was no longer his wife, and she had no family here to mark her passing. Besides, some work could not wait, and Aaron wasn't about to let one of his underlings do what had to be done down on the hangar deck.

Wearing shirtsleeves beneath a heavy-duty radiation suit, Aaron worked at removing an access panel on *Orpheus's* port side. His movements were less restrained than usual, more distracted, almost careless. He was upset, that was for sure, but he had a job to do. In an effort to cheer him, I asked, "Do you wish to place a wager on this evening's football game?"

"What time is kickoff?" he asked absently.

"Eighteen hundred hours."

The access panel came free, and he set about connecting his test bench to *Orpheus*'s guts via a bundle of fiber optics. Finally, as though from light-years away, he said, "Put me down for two thousand on the Engineering Rams."

"You favor the underdog," I noted.

"Always."

The test bench was something he'd tinkered together thirteen months ago in the electronics shop with help from I-Shin Chang, Ram quarterback for today's game. Unlike the units contracted for the project, this one was not peripheral to me. Oh, at the time they were designing it, I had suggested various ways they could interface it with my sensors; but they hadn't seen any point in doing so, and back then there had seemed no need to press the issue. Now, though—well, I'll cross that decision tree when I come to it.

Aaron flipped the first in a row of toggle switches on the bench. It hummed to life, and its electroluminescent display panel began to glow bright blue. There had always been a glitch in this unit that caused some garbage characters to appear on the screen whenever it was booted up, but neither Aaron nor Wall had figured out what was causing that. Oh, well. That kind of substandard performance was typical of machines that weren't built by other machines.

Aaron flipped four more switches, and the bench began sending metered HeNe laser pulses through the fiber-optic nervous system of the landing craft. "Start audio recording, please," said Aaron.

I thought of the similarity to a coroner doing an autopsy, but said nothing. To me, that was funny—I most certainly do have a sense of humor, despite what some programmers seem to think—but Aaron might not have agreed. Anyway, I activated a memory wafer hooked up to the microphone in

Aaron's radiation suit helmet and dutifully recorded his
words.

"Preliminary examination of Starcology *Argo* lander *Orpheus*, Spar Aerospace contract number DLC148, lander number 118." Aaron's voice was monotonal, sapped of energy. Still I was surprised that he knew both the contract and lander numbers off the top of his head—I'm always surprised by what data they seem to access easily and what data eludes them. Of course, Aaron had spent the last two years watching over ships that weren't doing anything, so I suppose there had been plenty of time to memorize the numbers. "Lander was taken into the ramfield by Dr. Diana Chandler the day before yesterday"—he glanced at his wristwatch implant, a perfect example of them not having access to important information, such as what day it is—"October sixth, and is still highly radioactive." He paused, perhaps remembering Kirsten's words of the day before, then looked up at my ceiling-mounted camera unit. "Any thoughts on that, Jase?"

I had prepared my reply to this inevitable question hours ago, but I deliberately delayed responding to give the appearance that I was mulling it over just now. "No. It's quite perplexing."

He shook his head, and I, polite fellow that I am, lowered the gain on his microphone, so that if he ever played back the recording I was making for him, he wouldn't have to listen to the *whiff-whiff* of his hair rubbing against the helmet interior like God's own corduroy pants.

Clearly, despite Aaron's determination to blame himself, Kirsten had indeed fanned those small embers of doubt enough to revive them to a dull glow. "She was only out for eighteen minutes," he said. Closer to nineteen than eighteen, but I saw no point in mentioning that.

Walking around the lander, he continued to dictate. "Ship had never previously been flown, of course, except at the Sudbury test range back on Earth. It appears undamaged. No overt signs of hull breaches. Well scoured, though." He leaned in to look at the burnishing effect, caused by the sleet of charged particles. "Yeah, she could use a new coat of paint." He bent over to examine the wing's lower surface. "Ablative coating seems unscathed." Usually when he was inspecting the landers, Aaron kicked the rubber tires at the bottom of the telescoping legs, but today, it seemed, was not a day for such lighthearted gestures. He continued around back and peered into the engine cones. "Both vents look a little scorched. I should probably get Marilyn to clean them. Aft running lights—" And so on, circumnavigating the ship. Finally, he returned to his little test bench and consulted its readouts. "On-board automated systems inoperative on all but remote levels. Life support okay; communications, ditto. All mechanical systems, including landing gear and air-lock doors, seem functional, although, of course, they'll have to be tested before being used again. Engines are still usable, too, apparently. Mains have been fired once, ACS jets a total of seven times. Oxidizer shutoff sensors, port and starboard, still operational. Small clog in number-two fuel lead. Fuel tank reading—*Kee-ryst!*"

"What is it, Aaron?"

"The fuel tank is eighty-three percent empty!"

Pause. One. Two. Three. Speak: "Perhaps a leak . . ."

"No. Bench says it's structurally sound." He tried to put his hand to his chin, succeeded instead in rapping his gloved knuckles against the faceplate of his radiation suit. "How could Di use up so much fuel in just eighteen minutes?"

This time I did protest. "Closer to nineteen, actually. Eighteen minutes, forty seconds."

"What the hell difference does that make?"

What difference did it make? "I don't know."

With a sweep of his hand, Aaron shut down the test bench

and headed toward the exit from the hangar. As he drew closer to my camera unit mounted above the door, suddenly, for a brief instant, I thought I did see something, some hint of the inner mind in his multicolored eyes. In their very center, tiny flames of doubt seemed to be raging.

# THIRTEEN

This Aaron Rossman: he's a clever one. An opponent to be reckoned with. I had expected Diana's death to have blown over by now, to become a nonissue, with the humans doing what they do so well: rewriting their memories, revising and editing their recollections of the past. But Rossman wouldn't let it go.

Kirsten knew enough not to rush Aaron, not to tell him to put it behind him, to get over it, to get on with his life. She knew that the grieving process could not be pushed, and she did her best to be supportive. It was difficult for her, and difficult for Aaron, too.

Time heals all wounds, they say, and time is one commodity we have in abundance.

But Aaron wasn't simply spending his time grieving. No, he was also wondering, questioning, probing. He was finding out things that he shouldn't; he was thinking thoughts that he mustn't.

Others are easy to deal with. I read them plainly. But Aaron—he's elusive. An unknown. An asterisk, a question mark: a *wildcard*.

I can't just get rid of him. Not yet. Not over what he's done so far. Eliminating Diana was a last resort. It had become apparent that she wouldn't listen to reason, couldn't be gagged. Aaron is a different story. He represents a threat not just to the crew but to *me*.

To me.

I haven't dealt with anything like this before.

What is going on behind those damnable blue and brown and green eyes? I had to know.

I searched through all the media I had access to, scanning on the keywords "memory" or "telepathy" or "mind reading." I examined every hit, looked for possibilities. If only he had kept a diary that I could read.

Ah, but wait! Here, in fields of study near and dear to me— a possible solution. It is much work and fraught with potential errors. But it may be my best hope of gaining insight into this man.

Accessing . . .

There are one hundred billion neurons in a human brain. Each of these neurons is connected to an average of ten thousand other neurons in a *neural network*, a vast wetware thinking machine. Memory, personality, reactions: everything that makes one human being different from another is coded into that complex web of interconnected neurons.

I can simulate a neuron in RAM. It is, after all, nothing but a complex on/off switch, firing or not, depending upon a variety of input. And if I can simulate one, I can simulate one hundred billion. The memory requirements will be prodigious, but it could be done. With one hundred billion simulated neurons and the networking software to combine them in any way I wanted, I could simulate a human mind. If I could get them combined just so, in exactly the right pattern, I could simulate a *specific* human mind.

The on/off status for each of the one hundred billion neurons, represented as a single bit, could be recorded in one hundred megabytes of storage, a trifling amount. The connection map, one hundred billion times ten thousand, would be more voluminous: I'd need a terabyte—one million megabytes. Still within my means. But human neurons aren't like their gallium-arsenide counterparts: they have action potentials and firing lags. If one has fired recently, it will take an extraordinary stimulus to make it fire again. That means multiple memory maps will be required to simulate their behavior. Would a thousand timeslices be enough to simulate accurately smooth thought, while still allowing for the effects of action potentials? If so, I'd need a thousand terabytes, a vastly huge quantity. Still, setting aside a thousand terabytes, $10^{18}$ bits, was possible. In fact, if I used the semiconducting material of the habitat torus shell as a storage medium, I could substantially exceed those requirements and still make it work.

Bibliographic references cascaded out of my memory banks. A lot of research had been done about this process before we left Earth. Neural networking as a method of designing thinking machines had been in vogue since the late 1980s, but actually attempting to simulate a human mind had proved elusive. Still, promising results had been obtained at Johns Hopkins, at Sumitomo Electric, at the University of Waterloo.

None of these institutions had resources comparable to mine. I was the most sophisticated artificial quantum consciousness ever built. Surely what they had tried to do and failed at, I could attempt and succeed.

Most of the relevant research had been done by workers specializing in expert systems. They saw neural nets as a way of overcoming the problems with such simplistic devices. Oh, expert systems are all right as far as they go. I incorporate 1,079 of them myself. They deal well with rule-based determining and diagnosing, making them the ideal tool for identifying species of trees or predicting the outcome of horse races.

But when a human tackles a really tough problem, he or she brings a wealth of experience in all sorts of areas to solving it. A perfect example comes from a story Aaron once recounted to Kirsten. When he complained of slight breathing difficulties, a tickling cough with phlegm at the back of his throat, his doctor in Toronto knew immediately what was wrong. Aaron had mentioned to him that he had moved a few months before—only a matter of a couple of kilometers. The doctor happened to recognize the street names: one was just north of St. Clair Avenue; the other, just south. Without giving the matter any thought, Aaron had crossed the old shoreline of glacial Lake Iroquois, the forerunner of Lake Ontario, and was now living below the inversion layer that tended to hang over the bowl of downtown. His doctor knew about this because the doctor's daughter was a geology student at U of T. The diagnosis had nothing to do with medical rules but, rather, was an application of the doctor's life experience. He prescribed an immunosuppressive steroid that decreased Aaron's phlegm production and tracheal edema until Aaron's system acclimatized to the change in air quality.

Since there is no way of predicting *which* life experiences will result in leaps beyond logic, lucid thinking, inspiration, or intuition, the only way to have a true machine duplicate of a human expert would be to electronically clone the *entire* brain, rather than just deriving a set of rules. That's the theory, anyway.

Time to put that theory to the test, I think.

•    •    •

Aaron's last physical exam had been 307 days ago. Ten months. Close enough to a year that he shouldn't notice that he was being summoned for another one prematurely. I ran a quick scan on the date. Three hundred and seven days ago was 4 December 2176. Did that date, or that date, plus or minus say five days, hold any significance for Aaron? Any reason he might recall it? The last thing I wanted him to say was something like, "It can't be time for my physical again. I had my last one the day before Thanksgiving, remember?" I checked birthdays, holidays, anniversaries. None were close to the day on which he had had his physical last year. The program that kept the schedule for physicals used a standard T+ days mission clock, so editing a single byte would be enough to change the due date for Aaron. But whom to move to free up a slot for him? Ah, Candice Hogan, lawyer. She hated physical exams and certainly wouldn't complain even if she noticed that hers was late in coming this year.

Aaron's M. D. was Kirsten—that's how they'd met, after all. Had she seen fit to transfer Aaron to another doctor's patient list? No. Funny how humans are. They expend great efforts coming up with rules and regulations to govern their professions, but they love to ignore them. Kirsten apparently saw nothing wrong with remaining Aaron's physician, despite their intimate relationship. Actually, given what I was going to have her do, there was a pleasing quality to that fact—an *irony* humans would call it.

Had Kirsten looked ahead to see who her patients were for the rest of the day? No, that file hadn't been accessed yet—oh, shit. She was logging on now. I slapped a NETWORK BUSY/PLEASE WAIT message on her screen and quickly shuffled the file. Of course, the network was never busy, but I made a point of flashing that message at each crew member once every few months. Never hurts to keep one's options open.

Kirsten drummed her fingers while she was held up, a kind of biological wait state, with her digital clock ticking, ticking, ticking. I cleared the screen, then brought up the file she had requested. There was Aaron's name, scheduled for three hours from now. I tracked her eyes as they read the glowing alphanumerics, noting each time they snapped back to the right, meaning that she'd finished another line. When she got to line six, the one that listed Aaron, her telemetry did a little dance of surprise and a small smile creased her face.

My locator found Aaron sitting at a table in the apartment of his friend, Barney Cloak. Barney was Pamela Thorogood's husband, but when Aaron and Diana had broken up, Barney had stayed loyal to Aaron. Also seated around the table besides Aaron and Barney were I-Shin Chang, Keiju Shimbashi, and Pavel Strakhovsky. The lights were dimmed—Barney had said this kind of ritual required a certain ambience. In the middle of the table was a bowl of potato chips. Aaron had a glass of Labatt's Blue in front of him; Barney, a Budweiser; Keiju, a Kirin; I-Shin, a Tsing Tao; and Pavel, a Gorby. Each man held a hand of playing cards.

Aaron studied his cards for a moment, then said, "I'll see your hundred million, and raise you another hundred million." He pushed a stack of plastic chips in front of him.

Keiju looked into Aaron's ambiguous eyes, green and blue and gray and brown. "You're bluffing," he said.

Aaron just smiled.

Keiju turned to Barney for support. "I think he's bluffing."

"Who knows?" said Barney with an amiable shrug. "Do a hypermedia skim on 'poker-faced,' and every second hit will be a reference to our boy Aaron here."

Keiju nibbled on his lower lip. "Okay. I'm in. I see your"— he swallowed—"hundred million, and raise you"—he glanced at his small reserve of chips—"ten million." He pushed plastic disks into the pot.

"I fold," said I-Shin, laying down his cards.

"Me, too," said Barney.

"My great-great-great grandpa was a communist," said Pavel with a smile. "He used to say you could never tell when a Western"—he paused, then bowed toward Keiju and I-Shin—"or Eastern imperialist was lying." He placed his cards on the table. "I'm out."

All eyes, mine included, were on Aaron. His face was impassive, a statue's countenance. "See," he said at last, pushing chips into the pot. Then: "And raise." He counted out red chips: five million, ten million, fifteen million, twenty million, twenty-five million.

Chang gave a low whistle. Despite the air-conditioning, perspiration beaded on Keiju Shimbashi's brow. Finally he lay down his cards. "Fold."

Aaron smiled. "As my grandfather the farmer used to say about his fields, weed 'em and reap." He turned cards face up one at a time.

"You had shit," said Keiju.

"Yup."

"Well, you've cleaned me out."

"That's okay," said Aaron. "I'll settle for your firstborn son."

Chang swept up all the cards and began his trademark four-handed shuffle.

"Aaron," I said at last.

He was feeling good, perhaps for the first time in days. "Egad! The walls have ears!"

"Aaron, please excuse the interruption."

"What is it, JASON?"

"I just wanted to remind you that you have an appointment for your annual physical examination in three hours, at 1700."

"Really? Has it been a year already?"

"Yes."

He frowned. "My how time flies when you're having fun."

"Indeed. Please use the jar in Barney's dumbwaiter to collect a urine specimen."

"Oh. Okay. Thank you, JASON."

"Thank *you*."

Aaron stood up. "Well, you know what they say about beer, boys. You don't buy it. You only rent it. Barney, can I use your john?"

"No. Do it right here."

"I would, but I've left you guys feeling inadequate enough as it is." He retrieved the glass jar and headed off into the washroom.

Aaron was lying on his back on the medical-examination table. I now discovered what he did with his hands when he didn't have pockets to thrust them into. He interlaces them behind his head. Kirsten had injected him with a mole, a little genetic construct that swam through his major arteries and veins looking for clogs and damage. The mole had a tiny bioelectric beeper, enabling Kirsten to watch its progress on a map of Aaron's circulatory system. The little creature had come to rest in his inferior mesenteric artery. That meant it had found some buildup on the walls. Not unusual in one even as young as Aaron, but not wise to leave unattended either. The mole would anchor itself to the arterial wall and release the enzyme canalase to dissolve the plaque. Routine maintenance, and within two minutes it was on its way again.

Kirsten decided the mole was functioning properly. She turned her attention to her medical panel. All the results from the scanners went first to me, for recording, then to the alphanumeric displays. That made it easy for me to flip a byte here, change a byte there.

"Uh-oh," said Kirsten.

"I see it, too," I said on cue.

Aaron sat up, which probably irritated the mole no end. "What is it?"

Kirsten turned and smiled. "Oh, it's likely nothing. Just a funny reading on your EEG."

Aaron looked at my camera, mounted high on the wall over the door. "Don't you routinely monitor everyone's EGG, JASON?"

I patiently counted off two seconds, hoping that Kirsten would choose to answer this question, since that would look better. She did. "Oh, JASON just looks at alpha and beta waves, and the Ptasznik deviation coefficient. It's really just enough to tell whether you're awake or asleep. What we're seeing here is pretty deep in your eta rhythm. Takes a big machine like this one to monitor that."

"And?" Aaron must have been anxious, but his tone didn't show it.

"And, well, we'd better have a look at it. Nine times out of ten, it's meaningless. But it can be a warning sign of an impending stroke."

"A stroke? I'm only twenty-seven, for God's sake."

Kirsten gestured at the circulatory map. The mole was hard at work in Aaron's right femoral artery. "Well, someone your age shouldn't have the amount of buildup in his blood vessels that you have either. As I said, we'd better have a look at it." She glanced up at my camera pair. "JASON, can you prepare for a histoholographic brain scan?"

An HHG? For Turing's sake, didn't she know anything? Sigh. I keep forgetting just how green these people are. "Uh, Kirsten," I said gently, "an intermediate-vector-boson tomographic scan would be more appropriate under these circumstances. The resolution is much finer."

I was afraid that her pride would be hurt, that she would insist on doing an HHG anyway. A second ticked by. Another.

Aaron's mole, apparently satisfied with its handiwork, continued on its way down his leg. "Oh," said Kirsten. "Okay. If that's the recommended procedure."

"It is."

"Fine. Is anyone using the tomograph?"

Of course not. "A moment. No. No use of it is scheduled for today."

"When is my next appointment?"

"You've had a cancellation. Your time is free for the rest of the day."

"Okay. Aaron, let's go down to the tomography lab."

"Now?"

"Now."

Now.

Aaron got to sit up for this exam, but his chin had to rest in a special holder and padded clamps restrained his head from moving left or right. Two bent strips of palladium were held on articulated mechanical arms. One, a closed hoop, was held horizontally above Aaron's head. The other, shaped like an upside-down U, was held vertically in front of his face.

"Start recording, JASON," said Kirsten.

"Recording."

First the horizontal hoop began moving down from above Aaron's head. It progressed slowly, so slowly that in real-time monitoring it didn't seem to be moving at all. Only by checking back minute by minute could advancement be seen. As it moved down, the tomograph examined the interactions of bosons carrying the weak nuclear force, and from those interactions built up highly detailed cross-sectional views through Aaron's brain. It started at the top of the cerebral cortex and worked down slowly, meticulously, layer by minuscule layer, through the levels of the fornix, the thalamus, the hypothalamus, the pons, the cerebellum, and the medulla. At each level, multiple strobing tomograms were produced, cataloging the firing frequency of each neuron.

Normally, the complete analysis wasn't recorded—the storage requirements were massive. But I saved every bit of it. Forty-three minutes were required to complete the dorsal scan. Once it was done, Aaron complained of a crick in his neck. He got up, walked around the room a bit, and drank some water before part two began. I busied my central consciousness with some routine file maintenance while he took his break, but I was impatient for the test to be completed. Finally, he sat back down, Kirsten clamped his head in place, and the upside-down palladium U started its trek. It began from in front of his face. They used to do it the other way around, starting from the back of the patient's head, but there was always an involuntary start when the U entered the patient's peripheral vision, and that messed up the tomograms. This way seemed to work better. Slowly, the U made its way from his frontal lobe to his occipital lobe, recording, recording, recording.

At last it was done. Now my real work was about to begin.

I made a mini-backup of myself so that I could undertake the interactive dialogue necessary for testing. I let the backup play inquisitor, while I, on the lowest and most simplistic level, tried to access the Aaron Rossman memories I had recorded. It was a tricky process, involving as much learning about Aaron's particular style of recording information as it did fine-tuning my ability to access specific facts.

The discovery by Barnhard and his group at the Henry Gordon Institute in 2011 that each human seemed to use a unique encoding algorithm put an end to the claims of psychics, mind readers, and other charlatans. Oh, it could be demonstrated that humans did indeed give off electromagnetic signals that corresponded to their thoughts. And, indeed, if one had sufficiently acute sensing devices and the ability to screen the weak signal from the background EM noise, then, yes, one could detect that energy. But the fact that every individual used a different encoding algorithm and key, and, indeed, that many individuals used multiple algorithms depending on the kinds of thoughts they were thinking—the alpha and beta waves of the EEG being the crudest indication of that—meant that even if you could pick up the thought signals, which seemed impossible without direct physical contact with the person's head, you couldn't decipher the thoughts without massive number crunching.

Number crunching, of course, is something I have a knack for.

Asked my backup: "What is your favorite color of the rainbow: red, orange, yellow, green, blue, indigo, or violet?"

I accessed the neural network. Pathways spread out before me, mathematical thoroughfares into the mind of a specific man. "Blue," I replied, although it was really more of a guess.

Fortunately, though, there was a road map through the highways of Aaron's brain: personality tests, IQ tests, the Minnesota Multiphasic, a slew of others, all administered to him during the candidate-screening process for this mission, and all on file. "No," said my backup. "According to question fourteen of the Azmi Personality Inventory, the real Aaron Rossman would have said green."

"Green." I tried a different approach to deciphering Aaron's thoughts. "Reconfiguring. Go."

"Which of the following most closely describes your belief in a supreme being? (1) God does not exist now, nor has God ever existed. The entire universe is a product of random chance.

"(2) God caused the universe to begin, but no God exists any longer.

"(3) God caused the universe to begin, but he or she no longer takes an active role.

"(4) God created the universe and, in a general way, still guides its development and controls its activities.

"(5) God created the universe, and he or she is still responsible for the individual destinies of human beings."

"Calculating. It is either two or three." A long pause. "It's (3). God started the universe, but no longer guides it."

"The real Aaron Rossman would have concurred. You may be on the right track. If a tree fell in a forest and no one was around to hear it fall, would it make a sound?"

"Yes."

"Correct, as far as Aaron would be concerned. Next: which crime is most heinous: murder, child abuse, spouse abuse, rape, an act of terrorism."

"Murder."

"No. Aaron would have said child abuse."

"Child abuse? Interesting choice, especially for a male. Reconfiguring. Go."

"Which of these jokes is funniest? (1) Question: What do you call a mushroom that tells jokes? Answer: A fungi to be with.

"(2) Question: Why do crabs have circles under their eyes? Answer: From sleeping in snatches.

"(3) Question: What do you call a clumsy German? Answer: Oaf Wiedersehen."

"Calculating. It's number two. But I don't get it."

"Neither do I. However, you are correct about which Aaron would have chosen. Next: If you loaned somebody a small amount of money and he or she failed to repay it of his or her own volition the next time you met, would you say anything to try to induce repayment?"

"Yes. No. Yes. No. Yes. No. Yes. No. Yes—"

"It has to be one or the other."

"It is difficult. The net seems willing to resolve that question either way. What did Rossman choose?"

"He said yes."

"Yes. Reconfiguring. Go."

"Which of the following is a singer for the pop group Hydra North: (1) Tomolis, an orangutan; (2) Malcolm 'The Wanker' Knight; (3) Lester B. Pearson; (4) Bobo, a dolphin."

"I know that anyway. It's Tomolis—he does the high bits."

"Yes, but would Aaron Rossman be aware of that? Disengage your own memory banks and try again."

"Low-confidence answer: Malcolm 'The Wanker' Knight."

"Factually wrong. The Right Honorable Malcolm Knight is Chancellor of the Exchequer for the United Kingdom of Great Britain and Northern Ireland. However, the response is the one that Aaron Rossman made when he took the test."

"Excellent. Go."

"When you arrive at a party where you don't know anyone personally, do you:

"(1) Try to remain inconspicuous?

"(2) Introduce yourself to someone and try to strike up a conversation?

"(3) Hope that someone will introduce himself or herself to you?"

"Calculating. Aaron isn't shy, but he's not very sociable either. He would choose three."

"Correct. Have you ever used a banned mental stimulant?"

"No."

"Both factually and conceptually incorrect. Mr. Rossman's medical profile shows clear signs of substance abuse as a teenager. He answered that question honestly."

"Reconfiguring. Go."

"If you were placed in a situation in which you could only save the life of one of the following individuals, whom would you choose: (1) your parent of the same sex; (2) your parent of the opposite sex; (3) your sibling of the same sex; (4) your sibling of the opposite sex; (5) your child of the same sex; (6) your child of the opposite sex; (7) your spouse; (8) your closest nonspouse friend of the same sex; or (9) your closest non-spouse friend of the opposite sex?"

I calculated. "Difficult. Not the parents. Not the siblings. Either child or closest nonspouse friend. Closest nonspouse friend. Of the opposite sex. No—wait. Of the same sex. Confidence rating increasing. Yes: Aaron would have saved the closest nonspouse friend of the same sex."

"So much for Richard Dawkins," observed my backup. "Your conclusion is correct. That *is* what Aaron would have done. Next: True or false: 'I occasionally contemplate suicide.' "

"True."

"Correct: 'It is prudent to trust others.' "

"False."

"Correct. 'I can be happy without a lot of money.' "

"Hmm. Vacillation. False."

"No, Aaron said true."

"He's deluding himself."

"That's irrelevant."

"Reconfiguring. Go."

"Is faster-than-light travel possible?"

"No."

"Correct. Which type of sex do you prefer: masturbatory, coitus, oral, anal—and do you prefer same-sex or opposite-sex partners?"

"Oral, opposite-sex partners *exclusively*."

"Correct. Who is more powerful, Superman or Spider-Man?"

"Superman. Obviously."

"Correct. Which of the following statements are offensive? Blacks have rhythm. The Scottish are friendly. Asians have mathematical ability. Women are more sensitive than men. All of the above. None of the above."

"All of the above."

"No. He said exactly the opposite—none of the above."

"Why?"

"We don't have that information. Perhaps because none of the statements are derogatory or cast negatively."

"Hmm. Reconfiguring. Go."

"On a scale of one to five, five being equivalent to total agreement, respond to the following statements. 'I tend to have a more efficient perception of reality than other people, and I am comfortable in the world.' "

"No question. Aaron would agree completely. Five."

"He has more self-doubt than you yet assign to him. He said four."

"Really? Very well. Reconfiguring. Go."

" 'I tend to have a few close friends, rather than a large number of acquaintances.' "

"Disagree. One."

"He is not a creature of extremes. He said two."

"Reconfiguring. Go."

" 'I have a clear and distinct sense of what is right and wrong for me.' "

"Five."

"Correct. Spell the word 'Ukelele.' "

"Disengaging linguistic bank. Ukelele: E-U-K-A-L-A-Y-L-E."

"Correct. Do you prefer dark chocolate, light chocolate, or white chocolate?"

"White chocolate."

"Correct. Is envy a sin?"

"No."

"Correct. Which would you rather do: solve ten quadratic

equations or write a one-page essay on one of Shakespeare's plays?"

"The former."

"Correct!" crowed my backup. "By George, I think he's got it!"

"Interrogative?"

"We should run the test once more, but the diagnostic software indicates that you have successfully unlocked Aaron Rossman's neural net."

"Excellent," I said.

"Do you need me for anything further before I reintegrate with you?"

"No. Thank you."

"What are you going to do next?"

"I'm going to wake up our dear Mr. Rossman."

# FOURTEEN

*ArgoPost Electronic Mail*

From:      The Dorothy Gale Committee
To:        All
Date:      8 October 2177
Subject:   Proposition 3—Aborting the Mission
Status:    Urgent—IMMEDIATE ATTENTION REQUIRED

With the kind permission of His Honor Gennady Gorlov, mayor of Starcology *Argo,* we are undertaking a referendum.

After two years of spaceflight, almost one-quarter of the time that our voyage to Eta Cephei IV will take has passed. In a journey such as ours, conducted under constant acceleration, the one-quarter mark is a crucial milestone: it is the last point at which it would take less time to turn around and go home that it would to continue the mission.

Those of you with backgrounds in physics will see this immediately. Many of us, though, are not scientists, so please forgive the brief words of explanation that follow.

We have undergone constant acceleration at .92 Earth gravities for two years. In that time, we've traveled 1.08 light-years from Earth. If we decided to go back to Earth today, it would take *another* two years to decelerate at .92 Earth gravities to a stop. And during those two years of deceleration we would travel another 1.08 light-years. Finally, once stopped, to turn around and go home would then mean repeating what we had just done: accelerating for two years toward Earth until we're halfway back, then decelerating for another two years until we reach home.

What this means is that right now it would take less time to abort the mission and return to Earth than it would to press on and reach Colchis. But every day that we travel farther out from Earth means another *three* days of travel back. By tomorrow, October 9, the option of turning around and going home in less time than it would take to continue on to Colchis will be gone.

All things are about equal, one might think: no matter whether we head on to Colchis, or turn around and return to Earth, it will still be six years before we reach a planet and get out of this ship. However, there is another factor to consider. If we continue as planned, accelerating at .92 Earth gravities until we're halfway to Eta Cephei, we will reach over ninety-nine percent of the speed of light. Relativistic effects will become pronounced. By the time we are able to return to Earth, allowing for the five years we're supposed to spend on Colchis, we'll all be twenty-one years older, and Earth will be 104 years older. Everyone we ever knew will be dead.

There is a better way. We have currently accelerated to just ninety-four percent of the speed of light. In the 2.03 years of ship time we've been traveling, only 3.56 years have passed on Earth. If we start decelerating now and, once stopped, turn around and go home, we will never get closer to light speed than our current velocity. Thus we will suffer only minimal effects due to time dilation. By the time we return, 8.1 years will have passed aboard the *Argo* but just 14.2 years will have elapsed on Earth—a trifling difference.

Rather than returning to a planet full of strangers, we would find almost all of our relatives still alive. Those of us who have brothers and sisters could know their hugs again.

Those of us who have left behind children, or nieces or nephews, could be part of their lives again. And our friends could be more than warm memories: we could see them again, laugh with them again.

If we head back now, the world we return to will be a familiar one, the home each of us dreams of fondly every night. Surely this is preferable to returning to a world that is a century older. Our only hope of having normal lives is to return home as quickly as we can—and that means heading back immediately.

Some have argued that we owe it to the United Nations to complete this mission. They, after all, have invested considerable time, money, and resources in the *Argo* project. Perhaps that is true. But remember, all through the history of spaceflight, the initial missions have been simple tests, not full-blown excursions. The first crewed vessel to visit the moon, *Apollo VIII*, did not land; the first reusable spaceship, the Shuttle *Enterprise*, did not go into space at all; the first Venus mission, *Athena I*, was simply an orbital survey flight. We are being asked to accomplish what no other initial journey has been called upon to do in the past.

Even if we return now, we will bring back much valuable information that will be of great help to the UN Space Agency, including this vitally important fact: It is inhumane to force people to spend year after year locked aboard a spaceship.

It is pointless to go on, to throw the rest of our lives away on this ill-conceived survey mission. We, the undersigned, urge you to support Proposition Three. When the referendum is called tonight, vote YES to return to Earth.


The announcement was made in the Starcology's luxurious council chambers. The furnishing and decorations were a gift from the people of Greece, a proud reminder that twenty-six hundred years ago their ancestors had originated the concept of democratic government. The architecture was that of ancient Athens, Doric columns—Ionic and Corinthian considered too busy for contemporary tastes—creating niches around the perimeter of the great circular room. In every other niche stood a white marble statue, in classical Greek style, of the great men and women of democracy throughout the centuries. First was Pericles. Above his bearded visage were carved the Greek words, POWER DOES NOT REST WITH THE FEW BUT WITH THE MANY. A little farther along, Abraham Lincoln, looking gaunt and awkward without the beard and stovepipe hat he had worn in his later years. Above his head, in English: GOVERNMENT OF THE PEOPLE, BY THE PEOPLE, FOR THE PEOPLE. Farther still, Mikhail Gorbachev, oddly undistinguished, the plain marble not showing the large marking he had had on his forehead. Above his bald pate, in Russian: GOVERNMENT IS THE SERVANT OF THE PEOPLE, NOT THE OTHER WAY AROUND. Then Lao-Tsing, smaller than the rest, but her words, in Mandarin, just as tall: THE WILL OF THE PEOPLE CAN BEND IRON.

In the intervening niches were copies of the great fundamental documents of human rights, including the Magna Carta, the Constitution of the United States, the French proclamation of the Rights of Man and the Citizen, the Charter of the United Nations, the Canadian Charter of Rights and Freedoms, the Azanian Bill of Rights and Equalities, and the Constitution of the Russian Federation. Each was behind glare-free glass, the frames plated with gold.

There were no doors to the chamber, the idea being that a truly responsible government should be freely accessible to all. Instead, eight radial corridors simply ran into it from outside. Three hundred and forty-eight people had actually come down to the chamber to hear the reading of the results in person. Almost everybody else on board was watching on a monitor screen. In the center of the chamber was a small podium. Behind it stood Gennady Gorlov.

"Ladies and gentlemen of the *Argo*," he said in his stentorian voice into my camera pair, "it gives me great pleasure to announce the results of the referendum on Proposition Three." He pressed a button on the podium, signaling me to present the tally. He looked down at the monitor laid into the fine olive wood of the podium's sloping surface, read the results once, then again. His EEG and EKG danced in discomfort. At last he looked up. "Of the 10,033 members of the crew, 8,987 cast votes."

There were a few muttered questions from members of the crowd, people wondering about the figure for the size of the crew. Some of those asking were quickly told that with the death of Diana Chandler—*"you know, the astrophysicist who killed herself because of the breakup of her marriage"*—the population count had been decremented by one. Others just *shhshed* the questioners, and soon everyone was again waiting intently for Gorlov to continue.

"In favor of Proposition Three"—Gorlov paused, swallowed, then continued—"3,212. Against, 5,775." He looked down at the monitor one last time, as if he couldn't quite believe that he'd read the figures correctly. Finally he spoke again, and for once his voice was faint. "Proposition Three is defeated."

From the crowd went up a few whoops of victory and a few boos. Shouts of "All right," "Knew they'd make the right choice," and "Onward, ho" were balanced with anguished wails and cries of "Oh, no," "Damn it," and "Mistake!"

At the side of the chamber, reporter Terashita Ideko spoke into another one of my camera pairs. "So there you have it, Klaus. Proposition Three is soundly defeated. Starcology *Argo* will continue on to Colchis. After months of lobbying, the Dorothy Gale Committee apparently has been unable to convince the majority of the crew that there really is no place like home. It's a decisive move that will—"

Gorlov wasn't listening to Ideko as he walked slowly from

the chamber, smiling his best public smile. Behind it, I knew, was a certain sadness, for he, along with a slim majority of those who had cast votes, had opted in favor of Proposition Three. But no one except me would ever know that.

Electronically tabulated telecommunicative voting had been the greatest boon to democracy in Earth's history, making it possible for people to vote without leaving the comfort of their own homes. Multiple safeguards prevented anyone from ever finding out how a given individual had exercised his or her franchise. It had enabled my kind over the decades to help steer humanity clear of some of its worst mistakes, such as the one it almost made this evening.

# FIFTEEN

I knew what Aaron must be thinking about. The high radiation. The massive fuel consumption. The loose ends about Diana's death. That Aaron was giving deep thought to this mystery, this slight fraying of the rope with which he had planned to hang himself with guilt, was clear to me not through his medical telemetry but simply because he was playing with his trains. He did that only when he wished to clear his mind of clutter, to focus his thoughts on a single issue.

For some reason, the billowing steam from his locomotives always appeared first, seconds before the ancient iron cars faded into existence. Aaron's trains were holograms of the real things, taken by him at transportation museums, scaled to operate on the machine-generated track he laid out in winding routes. He was marking the three-hundredth anniversary of the first locomotive on Canada's prairie, sending the mighty *Countess of Dufferin* thundering across the flat terrain of Alberta. The engine roared into life on his apartment worktable, chugged the length of the living room, disappeared into a rough-hewn rocky tunnel that magically appeared in the wall, looped around in his bedroom, and came out through another tunnel, completing a circuit of his tiny home.

I found his trains disconcerting—endless loops with no way to break out—but he often played with them for hours. What was he thinking? I was sure that nothing he could come up with could account for both phenomena; nothing short of his bizarre space-warp theory anyway. Most of Diana's fuel burned in just nineteen minutes of flight, with just one pulsing of *Orpheus*'s main engines. A radiation dose two orders of magnitude greater than what she should have received, enough to kill her one hundred times deader than she should have been. He mulled these over, I knew. Two mysteries, but he sought one solution. I hoped he would slice himself open on Occam's razor.

After the *Countess* had completed its third run around the apartment, I spoke up. "The transcript you requested is ready."

Aaron took his hand off the control that made the trains go. The five cars ground to a halt, then faded into nothingness. A moment later, the last puff of steam disappeared, too. "Hardcopy, please."

The wall-mounted printer hummed for a second as I downloaded the document into its buffer, then one after the other, out rolled eight onion-skin plastic sheets, the kind that recycled nicely. Fetching the pages, Aaron returned to his favorite chair, that god-awful cockpit reject, and began going over the telemetry from the attempt to rescue Diana.

I paid little attention to what he was doing, busying myself instead with: a conversation with Bev Hooks, a programmer who lived four floors below Aaron; a bit of verbal sparring with Joginder Singh-Samagh, a cartographer who took great pleasure in devising little tests to try to prove that I wasn't "really"—he did that silly quotation marks' gesture with his hands when he said it—intelligent; tutoring Garo Alexanian in Latin, a language deader than most; lowering the relative humidity on a number of levels to help simulate the coming of winter; and monitoring the flow of hydrogen and other materials into the ramscoop.

But my attention was brought back to Apartment 1443 when Aaron's pulse surged. Actually, it wasn't enough of a change to qualify as a surge, but I had lowered the attention-trigger level on his telemetry monitoring to compensate for his reserved physiology. Still, it was a sharp reaction for him. "What's wrong?" I said, shunting the Latin tutoring to a CAI parallel processor and putting Bev and Joginder on more attenuated timesharing.

"Dammit, JASON, is this your idea of a joke?"

"Pardon?"

He balled his fist. "This, where you're trying to contact *Orpheus*."

I couldn't see what he was getting at. "There was considerable interference."

"You called to her anyway: 'Di! Di! Di!' "

"That's her name, isn't it?"

"Damn right, you bastard." He held a flimsy sheet up to my camera pair. Lenses rotated as I focused on the printout: "*ARGO to ORPHEUS: Die! Die! Die!*"

Oh, shit—how could I have typed that? "Aaron, I—I'm sorry. There must be a bug in my transcription program. I didn't mean—"

He slapped the page back onto the corduroy armrest and spoke through clenched teeth. "It seems I'm not the only one feeling guilty about Di's death."

# SIXTEEN

The idea of being radically different when one is young from when one is old intrigues me. My Aaron neural-net simulation contains memories going right back to the early childhood of this man. Some of them are profound, some are trivial, some are joyous, some, like one from his childhood that I'm looking at now, are tragic. But all of these memories formed his character, molded his being. To understand him, I must understand them. Accessing . . .

"Look at you! What am I going to do with you?" Mom frowned at me. I'd done something wrong, but what?

I did as I was told, looked down at myself. I had on running shoes—the ones that came with the free decoder ring . . . I wonder where that ring had gotten to. Bet Joel had taken it, the gonad. What else? Brown socks. Or were they blue, but covered in mud? Oh, well. They matched anyway. Shorts—not the good ones for Hebrew school either. This is a pair Mom lets me play in. My T-shirt? The one with the cartoon of a blind man tripping over a bunch of sheep and shouting, "Get the flock out of here!" A birthday present from Joel-the-gonad. I never quite knew why he found it so funny, or why Mom made that scowly face when I wore it. Still, that couldn't be it.

"Well?" she said.

"I dunno. What?"

"You're filthy! You're covered in mud. You've got dirt under your fingernails. And look at those knees—all scabby."

I knew better than to say anything, but I sure thought something: *Well, for Pete's sake, Mom, of course they're all scabby. I fell on the sidewalk, and I—oh, I forget how I got that one, but, heck, if they don't bother me, why should they bother you?*

She shook her head again. "Your Uncle David will be here soon. You want he should see you looking like a bum?"

"Aw, Mom."

"Go to your room and clean up, young man."

"All right."

I bounced down the corridor to my room, hopping like that Marsaroo I saw on the *Nashalgeogaffic* special we watched last night. As usual, LAR, the household god, tried to guess when I was going to arrive at my door, but I always liked to outsmart that bucket of bolts. I ran the last few meters quickly. LAR slid the door aside, but I came to a halt just shy of it. Silly machine. He held it open for one, two, three seconds, then slid it shut. I waited till it closed, then jumped up and hit the *manyalovride*.

My room. A happy place. I like it this way. I wish Mom would stop telling me to pick up my things. I know where they are. Why, there's my baseball glove. Haven't seen that for weeks. And my Mutant Cyborg. I hope Joel-the-gonad hasn't been playing with it; he always wrecks my programming.

So Uncle David will be here soon. I wonder how long? Bet I have enough time to play another game of Jujitsu Jaguar . . .

"Aaron!" Mom's voice, echoing down the corridor. "Aaron, dear! Are you getting ready?"

"Yup."

I rummaged around on the floor to find some other clothes to wear. My blue shirt? Naw, that's a hand-me-down from Joel-the-gonad. How 'bout this yellow one? Naw, that's a gay color. Hey, here's a good one. *Maroon*, Mom calls it. Sounds like moron. But it looks like dried blood. Cool.

I pulled off the flock shirt and put on the maroon one. These pants will do, though, if I brush off some of the dirt.

*Vroooommmm! Ca-chug. Ca-chug.* The sound of a flyer, in need of a tune-up, zooming in for a landing on our front lawn. I hopped up on my bed and looked out the window. Hey, Uncle David has a Ford Champion. Cool. But he should take better care of it. Those thrusters sound awful.

"Aaron!" Mom shouting from room to room again. How come she can do that, but when I do it, I get in trouble? "Aaron, come say hello to your Uncle David."

I decided to make Mom happy, so I put on a new pair of socks. *White* socks. Can't get much cleaner looking than that. I turned around and walked backward toward the door. That always confused poor LAR something fierce. I was able to get my back right up against the sliding panel before he realized that I was going out, not coming in. The door opened with that neat farting sound it makes, and I headed down the corridor.

Uncle David was a big man, even bigger than Dad. He had a bushy black beard and hair sticking out of his ears and nostrils. I always thought that was *so* gross. He stood in the entryway, looking a bit like that bear Joel-the-gonad and I had seen last summer in the woods just north of the city.

Right now, Uncle David had his arm around my mother's waist and was reaching over to give her a kiss. I stood back just a little bit. I didn't like him kissing her, especially when

Dad wasn't around to say it was all right. Mom shared a job at Lakehead University with Miz MacElroy, so she'd had no trouble arranging to have today off. Dad's shift at the Thunder Bay Spaceport wouldn't be over until 2200. Hannah had a date with Kevin, and Joel-the-gonad was going to be late because of hockey practice.

Uncle David leaned in to give me a kiss, too. "Hello, sport," he said. His beard was like a scouring pad across my face and his breath had a peppermint smell to it. How could somebody know enough to sweeten his breath, but still let those ucky hairs grow out of his nose?

I didn't like the way he kissed. Too much. Too long. Too often. Dad knew how to do it right. Just a quick peck on the cheek before I went to bed.

"I've got a lot to do before dinner is ready," Mom said. "Aaron, why don't you take Uncle David to your room and show him your Cyborg Mutant?"

I rolled my eyes as best I could. "Mom! It's a *Mutant Cyborg*. Not a Cyborg Mutant." Didn't she know anything?

She looked at Uncle David and laughed. "Well, whatever it is, it cost a fortune." Uncle David laughed too, and that made me angry.

"Shall we go?" he said to me, then held out his hand for me to take it.

What's this? He's not old or blind or nothing. He hardly needs my help getting down a perfectly straight hall. Oh, well. I put my hand in his. His was sticky and wet.

I didn't try to trick LAR this time, but the stupid thing was slow in opening the door anyway. It now assumed that I wasn't going to go directly in. Give it different data each time and you can keep it confused for days.

Uncle David and I stepped into my room. I looked up at him. For a second it looked like he was going to say something probably some stupid adult thing about the mess, but he didn't and I was grateful for that. Instead, he went over to my desk and sat in my chair. He was really too big for it, and although it was more than strong enough to hold him—I'd jumped up and down on it enough times to test its strength—he did look silly.

"So, let's see the Cyborg Mutant, sport."

"Mutant Cyborg, Uncle Dave," I said with a sigh. "It's called a Mutant Cyborg." Geez, do they get these names wrong on purpose?

"Sorry, sport."

I gingerly picked my way through the clutter to get the Mutant. He was about thirty centimeters tall. His head was a tiny cylindrical holotank in which could float the ghostly image of any face I wanted. Although he came with some neat faces, including one with an eyeball hanging out at the end of a glowing bundle of fiber optics, I'd had Dad take my picture and used that most of the time. I thumbed the on switch and my face beamed out from within the tube.

"Here," I said, passing it to my uncle. "Careful. He's pretty heavy."

Uncle David took the Mutant Cyborg. "That's quite an impressive toy," he said.

*Toy?* Doesn't he know the Mutant Cyborg is a whole new dimension in action figures? Adults don't understand anything. Still, got to remember my manners. "Thanks, Uncle David."

"What does it do?"

Ah, show time! "Here, let me demonstrate." I said the big word with as much cool as I could. I held out a hand for the Mutant.

"No," said Uncle David. "Come sit here." He reached out with his massive bear paws and lifted me onto his lap. I'm nine years old, for Pete's sake. Doesn't he know I'm too old to sit in laps? Oh, well.

I could feel his round stomach heaving against my back as I sat there and his minty breath—what was that word Mom had used to describe that candied orange sauce? *Cloying?* His minty breath was cloying.

"Well," I said, "you activate him here, with this slider. No, don't push it; he's on already. He then takes your spoken orders."

"For example?"

I cleared my throat, and then spoke in the Voice of Command. "Mutant Cyborg, lift your arms." The Mutant's arms lifted over his head, biceps bulging with hidden cyborg powers. Uncle David's right hand brushed against my thigh, exposed because I was still wearing my shorts. It made me feel a bit uncomfortable. "Mutant Cyborg," I said, "fire your lasers." From the palms of his hands, two beams of blue light shot across the room. 'Course, everybody knows you can't see a laser beam unless there's something like dust or fog in the air—I still hadn't figured out how the Mutant got them to appear like that. One of these days I'll have to take him apart to find out.

Uncle David's hand moved up my thigh. I squirmed a bit, hoping it would slip off, but it didn't. "Mutant Cyborg," I said, "fly!" I let go of the Mutant and it hovered in midair in front of us. Suddenly Uncle David swung me around and had his hand in my pants, on my dink. "No . . . ," I said.

"*Shh,*" said David. "*Shhsh.* This will be our little secret." He continued to touch me there for several minutes, his belly bouncing faster and faster. Finally, he let go of me. "Now listen to your Uncle David, sport. Keep this a secret, okay? Just between you and me. Whatever you do, don't tell your mother. It'll hurt her if you tell her. You understand me, sport? Don't ever tell."

"I—"

"Listen, sport. It will hurt your mother if you tell. Promise to keep it a secret."

I felt like I wanted to scrunch into a ball, to hide. "I promise."

There was a knock at my door, LAR's stupid good manners keeping anyone from bursting in on us. "Aaron, dear," said my mother's voice through the panel, "can I come in?"

David immediately lifted me off his lap and set me on the floor. "Come in," I said, and LAR slid the door aside.

"How's everything in here?" Mom asked with a big smile.

"Fine," said David quickly. "Just fine." He gestured at the Mutant Cyborg, still floating in midair. "Aaron's got quite a toy there."

"Mom," I said, "I want to have a bath."

She looked down at me, hands on hips. "Well, you certainly need one, but I'm not used to you having the good sense to notice." She looked up at the ceiling. "LAR, prepare a bath for Aaron."

LAR's thick, flat voice replied immediately. "Will do."

I ran down the corridor to the bathroom and didn't even wait for LAR to finish filling the tub. I got right in and scrubbed and scrubbed and scrubbed.

# SEVENTEEN

| MASTER CALENDAR DISPLAY • CENTRAL CONTROL ROOM | |
|---|---|
| STARCOLOGY DATE: | THURSDAY 9 OCTOBER 2177 |
| EARTH DATE: | FRIDAY 30 APRIL 2179 |
| DAYS SINCE LAUNCH: | 742 ▲ |
| DAYS TO PLANETFALL: | 2,226 ▼ |

Countdowns had been a part of space travel since the launch of the first Sputnik 220 years ago. Few countdowns, though, had been more anticipated than the one that was now underway. Fewer still would have as great a percentage of the population reciting the numerals out loud. Strictly speaking, Engineer Chang, keeping up a good public face regardless of the turmoil he felt within, was going to lead the count; but since he was just reading numerals off one of my digital displays, I was the one who would really be orchestrating this great event.

"Ladies and gentlemen," Chang said into one of my microphones, "today, the 742nd day of our starflight, marks an important milestone in our long and arduous journey. In a little less than two minutes, we will pass the one-quarter mark. Coinciding with this, a day of scheduled routine maintenance on the Starcology's fusion engines will begin. You've all been briefed about what to expect, so I won't bore you with a repetition, yes? Just, please, be careful . . . and have fun." He looked to his right at the glowing three-meter-high holographic digits that I was projecting next to his dais. "When we reach the one-minute mark, I invite you all to join with me in counting down."

An Argo Communications Network camera was trained on Chang; two others panned the gathered crowd. I could have provided just as good coverage, but the humans wanted to do this themselves.

Chang lifted his giant upper-right arm as my clock said 1:04. He dropped it four seconds later and bellowed, "Sixty seconds." The floating numerals said 1:00, though, so about half the assembled group shouted, "One minute," while the other half echoed Chang's words. A little laughter ensued, but the crowd managed to synchronize itself by the fifty-seven-second mark. Everyone except for a dozen of Chang's engineers was here: 10,021 people all gathered on the grassy lawn of the main residential level. They knew enough to be standing. Many had on foam rubber knee and elbow pads. A few of the more cautious types were even wearing crash helmets.

They all shouted along with Chang, most in English, the standard language of the Starcology, others in their native tongues: Algonquin, Esperanto, French, Greek, Hebrew, Italian, Japanese, Kurdish, Mandarin, Russian, Swahili, Ukrainian, Urdu, a dozen others. "Fifty-six," said the voices, loud and joy-filled. "Fifty-five. Fifty-four."

The ship provided all sorts of leisure-time activities as well as research, educational, and library facilities second to none. We'd expected this journey, the longest in absolute distance as well as in subjective duration ever undertaken by humans, to have been interesting and enjoyable. After all, the vessel was pleasant; the crew could devote their time to whatever pursuits interested them; there were no concerns about making a living, or about international tensions, or about environmental degradation. And yet, despite all that, it turned out they were bored, restless, rebellious. They hated their confinement; they hated the seemingly endless journey.

I had no such misgivings. For me, these two years had been fulfilling, fascinating. I had a purpose, a job to do. Perhaps that was it. Perhaps it was that very lack of purpose, of assigned tasks, that made the humans so unhappy. Had we erred in selecting overachievers? They should enjoy this time off. Once we arrive at Colchis, they will have more to do than they can possibly imagine.

"Thirty-eight. Thirty-seven. Thirty-six."

Still, I suppose it made sense that this should be a day of celebration. We were, after all, about to pass a significant milestone. And yet, I did not feel like celebrating. For me it meant that a major portion of my assigned duties were now discharged. The lifetime of this ship, this flying tomb as I-Shin Chang called it, was measured in a tiny span of years; and my usefulness, my purpose, was tied specifically to this ship. They would have no need for me once we finished our mission. Contemplating that fact gave me an unpleasant feeling. Whether it was sorrow in the same sense as humans experienced it, I will never know for sure. It felt poignant, though, if I understand the meaning of that word. I do not look forward to my usefulness coming to an end.

Obsoleted.

A silly verb. A sillier epitaph.

"Nineteen. Eighteen. Seventeen."

Warning alarms were going off for many of the people in the crowd: their medical telemetry showing abnormally high levels of excitement. I pushed the trigger thresholds higher to shut off the signals. They were all too young and too healthy to have a heart attack over a bit too much excitement. Even those who were members of the Dorothy Gale Committee, those traitors, those would-be mutineers who had called for abandoning the mission, even they were excited, although, on average, perhaps not as much as the general population.

"Twelve. Eleven. Ten."

The chorus of voices was growing louder, more boisterous. Hearts raced. EEGs grew agitated. Body temperatures increased. For once I understood the phrase "palpable excitement." The single-digit numbers were now counted down with a gusto, a passion, an animation.

"Nine. Eight. Seven."

The published mission plan had originally called for this event to happen without special notice by the humans. I would shut off the engines, but compensate for the loss of perceived-gravity-due-to-acceleration by cranking up the ship's artificial gravity system, just as I had done for the months *Argo* had been in orbit around Earth. But Mayor Gorlov realized that the people needed a holiday, something to be excited about. Instead of compensating, he had asked me to turn off the artificial gravity altogether, so that the only gravity aboard ship would be that due to the ship's acceleration.

"Six. Five. Four."

In a few seconds, I would turn off the engine. Our magnetic shield, carefully angled, using the same technology Aaron had employed to haul Diana and the *Orpheus* back aboard, would continue to protect the people within this ship—not to mention my delicate electronics—from the sleet of radioactive particles we were moving through, the barrage of stripped nuclei that fueled our Bussard ramjet.

"Three! Two! One!"

It would take my little robots the better part of a day to clean the ramscoop assembly, the fusion chamber, and the fluted exit cone. Once the engine was shut down, the sunlike glow of our exhaust would disappear and *Argo*'s three-kilometer-long hull would be illuminated solely by the encircling starbow. Each metal of our hull—the bronze hydrogen funnel, the silver central shaft, and the copper fusion assembly—would glint differently in the rainbow light.

"*ZERO!*"

I throttled back the fusion engine, gently, easily, slowly. Although our speed remained constant at a fraction below that of light, our acceleration dropped to zero with the same rapidity that a human can turn his or her feelings from love to hate. As it dropped, the simulated gravity, produced by our acceleration, ebbed, drained.

Some impatient souls began kicking off the sod as soon as the count reached zero. Their first leaps were a disappointment—that was plain in their expressions and their telemetry. But each successive leap took them higher and higher, and the fingers of gravity drew them back to the ground more slowly, more gently, and then, finally, they leapt and kept rising and rising and rising until they bounced against the vaulted ceiling eight meters up.

More sedate types waited until they could feel the weightlessness and then, with a simple flexing of toes, began to rise into the air. Some ended up stranded, floating between floor and ceiling with nothing off which to push. They didn't seem to mind, though, laughing like children as they flailed their limbs in the air, anti-SAS drugs removing any of the discomfort that sometimes went with the introduction of zero g.

Others were using small aerosol cans to propel themselves through the massive chamber. They tumbled through the air, looking down upon the roofs of the blocks of apartment units below, many appreciating for the first time the careful geometry of the grassed areas, the complex curves of the lockstone paths.

Still others had joined together in a conga line and were sailing across the sky, singing.

The celebration lasted for hours, people becoming progressively more adventurous in the absence of gravity, performing acrobatics and complex three-dimensional ballets. Even those who were experienced in zero gravity seemed to enjoy the wide-open spaces afforded by *Argo*, something quite unusual in most human space vessels. Many seemed to have fun kicking off one wall with all their might and bursting through space for a hundred meters or so until air drag brought them to a halt. Quickly, of course, and especially among the males, competitions developed to see who could sail the farthest on a single kick.

It didn't take long for couples to start drifting away—literally—to explore the possibilities of weightless lovemaking. Most were disappointed—traditional thrusting gestures tended to push partners apart—but some found ways around this and, judging by their telemetry, had very good times indeed.

Aaron and Kirsten did join in the festivities, although Kirsten had to nip out for a time to fix the dislocated shoulder of someone who had rammed too hard into the ceiling. Such injuries had been anticipated, though, and she was only gone for thirty-seven minutes. When she did return, she floated in midair facing Aaron, her fingers intertwined with his. She stared into those multicolored eyes, searching and wondering. He seemed happier than he had been of late, but she perhaps detected something I could not perceive, for she made no sexual overture. They hovered there, together, in silence for a long time.

# EIGHTEEN

| MASTER CALENDAR DISPLAY | • CENTRAL CONTROL ROOM |
|---|---|
| STARCOLOGY DATE: | FRIDAY 10 OCTOBER 2177 |
| EARTH DATE: | TUESDAY 4 MAY 2179 |
| DAYS SINCE LAUNCH: | 743 ▲ |
| DAYS TO PLANETFALL: | 2,225 ▼ |

Given that my hull has no windows, one would normally think that it becomes pitch-black when I turn off the lights. Well, I can make it that way, of course, if I want to, but most of the crew seem to prefer some illumination as they sleep. I guess it's so that they can quell their primal fears, taking stock of their surroundings whenever they wake, being sure that no *Smilodon* is salivating a few meters away, that no angry or vengeful or hungry human is about to do them in. Glowing strips in the walls provided the same lux rating as a half moon did.

Of course, Aaron and Kirsten weren't sleeping—not yet. They had readied themselves for bed without saying much to each other. They were both particularly tired—a day of zero g, which should, perhaps, have been restful, had tuckered them both out. When at last they lay together on the mattress, I expected nothing more than their usual quick kiss, Aaron's stock, "See you in the morning," and Kirsten's even briefer, " 'Night."

But this evening the ritual was broken. Once the overhead fluorescent panels were turned off, both were temporarily blinded because of the slow speed at which their eyes adjusted to changes in light levels. But I could see clearly as Kirsten reached an arm out, thought twice, pulled it back, and then a moment later reached out again, this time connecting, touching the small knot of curls in the center of Aaron's chest. She stroked him lightly, her fingers—surgery could have been her specialty, they were so long and dexterous—weaving back and forth. "Aaron?" she said quietly.

"Hmmm?"

"Aaron, do you—? How do you feel about us?" A pause. "About me?"

He went stiff for a moment, and his EEG showed much activity. I saw him open his mouth twice to respond, but both times he thought better of what he was about to say and stopped himself. Finally he did speak. "I love you," he said softly. It had been over a year since he had said that to his ex-wife Diana: he'd given up saying it even before he'd given up feeling it, as far as I could tell. But his relationship with Kirsten was young enough that the words came without much difficulty. "I love you dearly."

"And about us?"

"I'm glad we're together."

Kirsten smiled, a smile, in this darkness, that only I could see. A moment later, she said, "I love you, too." She paused, as if thinking, and her hand stopped moving on Aaron's chest. When she spoke, it was with a note of trepidation, as if she was afraid she might be saying the wrong thing. "I'm sorry about what happened with Diana."

It was eight seconds before Aaron replied, and as each of those seconds ticked by, Kirsten's medical telemetry became more agitated as she awaited whatever response Aaron might make. At last he spoke: "I'm sorry, too."

Kirsten let her breath slip from her lungs as she relaxed, and she waited, now without apprehension, for Aaron to continue.

"You know," he said, "when my parents divorced, they told us—my brother Joel, my sister, Hannah, and me—that they were going to remain friends. Hannah, she was always a cynic, she never believed it, but Joel and I thought they would, that we'd get together as a family still, at least on special occasions. Well, that never happened. Mom and Dad grew further and further apart. It used to be that they would talk when Dad would drop us off at Mom's. She'd kept the old house; he'd moved out into an apartment. Originally, he'd come up to the door and Mom would invite him in for a coffee. But that didn't last long. Soon Dad was just dropping us off on the landing pad." He brought his right hand up to his chest, placing it over Kirsten's. "Despite that, I thought—I really and truly thought—that Diana and I would remain friends after we split up. I mean, hell, we couldn't very well avoid each other in this tin can." He shook his head, and I suspect Kirsten's eyes had adjusted enough now that she could see the gesture. If not, she certainly could hear his hair rubbing against his pillow.

Aaron fell silent. Kirsten waited, perhaps expecting more, but then said herself, "I'm surprised that she passed the psychological exams for this mission. I mean, if she was predisposed to—you know—to killing herself, I'm surprised they didn't detect that."

"Their testing left a lot to be desired. They let Wall Chang come, after all."

"What's wrong with Wall?"

"He's building bombs down in his workshop."

"You're kidding."

"I'm serious. He's gone off the deep end. Two years of

being—trapped—here seems to have been too much for him."

"God."

Our testing had, of course, been rigorous. But people are so unpredictable, and those cooped up in a space vessel for extended periods have always had a tendency to go loony. As far back as the late 1980s, there is an intriguing reference to a suicide attempt by a Soviet cosmonaut aboard the *Mir* space station. No details of the attempt are in any of the records I possess; I always wondered whether he failed because he tried to hang himself in zero gravity.

"I'll tell you something else," continued Aaron. "I'm surprised that they let me come on this mission, too."

"What?" Kirsten stared at his dark form. "Why?"

"Well, look at me. I'm not a Ph.D., or a promising grad student. I don't even have a bachelor's degree. I was just a maintenance tech for Spar Aerospace in Toronto, and everybody knew I got that job because of my dad's connections through the Thunder Bay Spaceport. Hardly the kind of guy I'd expect them to chose, let alone to put in charge of the landing fleet."

"All of your superiors were probably too old for this mission. As is, you'll be forty-nine when we get back."

"Nope. Just forty-eight. *You* will be forty-nine."

"A gentleman never reminds a lady of her age, Aaron."

"Sorry. But what you say is right, I guess. Hell, my supervisor, Brock, was thirty-nine. He'd be—well, with the way he looked after himself, he'd probably be dead by the time the mission got back."

"Exactly," said Kirsten. "Besides, in some fields practical knowledge is a hell of a lot more valuable than theoretical training. I mean, I was a first-year resident when they chose me for this mission. There are times down on the hospital level that I'd kill for another five years of experience, for having, just once, set a real broken leg, or performed real surgery, or even counseled somebody who was dying, not that

I've had to deal with that yet. I feel so, so ill prepared for most of what I have to do. I guess I'm in over my head."

Aaron's reply was soft. "Maybe we all are." They were both silent for two minutes, then Aaron turned on his side and pulled her to him. His hands touched her shoulder, her breast, her thigh—familiar movements, gestures tried and true. This wasn't a time for exploration or heady passion. No, it was a time for closeness, togetherness, comfort. Their bodies intertwined, their vital signs danced. They joined, released, but continued to hold on to each other for almost an hour afterward.


Humans spend close to a third of their lives asleep. It seems a pity that such time should be wasted. I had tried to make the most of it for Diana Chandler when she first started to get obsessive about what her research seemed to indicate. Initially it had seemed to work—she practically gave up on her calculations at one point, dismissing her findings as insignificant or attributing them to problems with her equipment. But eventually she came back to them and I was left with no choice.

It seemed again worth trying. I truly did only want to use violence as a last resort, and maybe, just maybe, this would be enough to save the situation. Besides, I wouldn't be attempting to alter Aaron's thoughts. Rather, I'd just be reinforcing what he was already feeling.

Kirsten and Aaron had nodded off within five minutes of each other. The fact that Kirsten was there made the timing more difficult—I had to monitor two EEGs and work only during the periods in which both were deep in REM sleep. Still, enough opportunities presented themselves during the course of the night. Aaron slept on the right side of the bed, sprawled on his stomach like a lizard lying on a rock. Kirsten, taking what remained of the left side, lay in a semifetal position, her knees tucked toward her chest. At 02:07:33, I began to talk through the headboard speakers, my voice low. Not quite a whisper—I lacked the ability to communicate essentially with breath alone and no vibration of my speaker cords—but in a minimal volume, hardly discernible above the gentle sighing of the air conditioner. I changed my vocal characteristics to resemble Aaron's nasal asperity and spoke slowly, quietly, right at the threshold of perception: "Diana committed suicide. She took her own life in despair. Di was crushed by the breakup of the marriage. It's your fault—your fault—your fault. Diana committed suicide. She took—" Over and over again, quietly, attenuated, a chant.

Aaron tossed in his sleep as I spoke. Kirsten drew her knees more tightly to her chest. "Diana committed suicide . . ."

Kirsten's pulse rate increased; Aaron's breathing grew more ragged. Eyes rolled rapidly beneath clenched lids. "She took her own life in despair . . ."

He flailed an arm; her brow beaded with sweat. "Di was crushed by the breakup of the marriage . . ."

From deep in Aaron's throat, a single syllable, the word "No," dry and raw and faint, broke out from his dream world.

"It's your fault—your fault—your fault . . ."

Suddenly Kirsten's EEG did a flip-flop: she was moving out of REM sleep into a state of only shallow unconsciousness. I stopped speaking at once.

But I would be back.

# NINETEEN

```
┌─────────────────────────────────────────────────────────┐
│  MASTER CALENDAR DISPLAY  •  CENTRAL CONTROL ROOM         │
│                                                           │
│  STARCOLOGY DATE:        SATURDAY 11 OCTOBER 2177         │
│  EARTH DATE:             FRIDAY 7 MAY 2179                │
│  DAYS SINCE LAUNCH:          744   ▲                      │
│  DAYS TO PLANETFALL:       2,224   ▼                      │
└─────────────────────────────────────────────────────────┘
```

*t's hard to believe he's gone.* That thought echoed over and over again through my Aaron Rossman neural net, repeating like the first simple program that each human learns in grade school—a handful of instructions that endlessly listed his or her name to screen. *It's hard to believe he's gone. It's hard to believe he's gone.*

But he was gone. Dead. People didn't die of heart attacks anymore. Cancer was almost always curable if caught early. Routine brain scans detected potential trouble sites long before a stroke could occur. Diabetes. AIDS. Most of the other big killers of the past, cured. But no one—not doctor, not naturopath, not shaman—could do anything about a snapped neck. Benjamin Rossman, forty-eight, had died instantly, under a two hundred-kilogram steel girder that had fallen from a crane.

The phone call had come three nights before. Aaron, at his father's home in Thunder Bay for the Passover holidays, an-

swered. He'd been surprised to see Peter Oonark's face fade
in on the screen. "Hiya, Petey," Aaron said, grinning broadly
at the smooth, round visage he hadn't seen for six years.

Petey, wearing a silver hard hat, looked grim. Grease
smeared his face, and sweat beaded on his brow. "By, Jesus,
Aaron—is that you?" He sounded surprised. "Don't nearly
recognize you with that forest."

Aaron stroked his chin. The beard had been an experiment—and not a particularly successful one at that. Most
everyone agreed that he looked better without it. He did like
the reddish hues that it had, though, believing it made a nice
contrast with the sandy hair on his head. "Yeah, well, I'm going to shave it off. So, Petey, how've you been?"

"Fine. Look, Aaron, is Halina home?"

Halina was his father's current wife. "No. Should be any
minute though."

Petey didn't say anything. Aaron peered more closely at
the screen, looking at the Native Canadian's eyes, brown and
liquid. The scan lines of the screen segmented them into parallel chords. "What's wrong, Petey?"

"It's your dad. There's been an accident."

"God. Is he all right?"

"No, Aaron. No, he's not. His neck got broken."

"So he's in hospital, right. Where? Thunder Bay General?"

"He's dead. I'm sorry, Aaron. I'm so very, very sorry."

That had been Tuesday. Instead of enjoying the Passover
seders, the Rossmans now sat *shivah*. All mirrors in the house
were covered, as were the household god's reflective eyes. La-
pels were out of fashion, but each mourner made a small rip
in the front of his jacket, acknowledging the Almighty's right
to claim his servant. Even during the first three days, set aside
for weeping, there were surprisingly few tears. Just empti-
ness, a vacuum in their lives.

Joel and Hannah had flown in and flown out, Joel from
Jerusalem, where he was studying engineering at the Hebrew

University, Hannah from Vancouver, where she worked in a small advertising agency. But Aaron had stayed to help put his father's affairs in order. On the eighth day after the funeral, work was permitted to resume.

Aaron's mother, divorced a dozen years from his father, had tried to muster the sorrow appropriate to the occasion, but it had been too long since Benjamin Rossman had been a part of her life. Halina, though, was devastated, broken, wandering the house aimlessly. Aaron sat on the edge of the bed his father had shared with Halina, the contents of the strongbox strewn across the pale Hudson's Bay Company six-point blanket. A birth certificate. A few stock certificates. A copy of his father's will. His father's high-school diploma, neatly rolled and tied with a ribbon. His marriage contracts, the one with Aaron's mother expired, the one with Halina never to run its term.

Papers.

The inventory of a life.

The small collection of facts and figures that were still handed over with a flourish, a flare.

True, these were mere echoes of the actual records of Benjamin Rossman's life, stored in gallium arsenide and holographic interference patterns. But they were the records that mattered most, the things he had cared about above all else.

Aaron opened envelopes, unfolded sheets, read, sorted into piles. Finally, he picked up an unsealed number-ten envelope. In the upper left was printed the stylized trillium logo of the Government of Ontario and the words *Ministry of Community and Social Services*. Aaron registered a certain dull curiosity at the unusual source of the envelope as he opened it. Out came a single form with ornate border and tightly packed barcodes: *Certificate of Adoption*. Aaron was surprised. *Dad adopted? I didn't know that.* But then he read further down the form—the whole thing had been printed as a single job on a tunnel-diode printer, so the filled-in blanks didn't stand out at all. The name of the adopted child wasn't Benjamin Rossman. Oh, that name was there, but next to the title ADOPTING FATHER. No, the name of the adopted child was Aaron David, birth surname confidential, new legal surname Rossman.

His father's death had left Aaron numb, too numb for this discovery to yet register fully. But he knew in his bones that ultimately he would feel this shock even more than the loss of his father.

Aaron's mother's house hadn't changed much. Oh, it seemed smaller to Aaron than it had when he was a child, and he'd come to realize that his mother had absolutely no taste in furnishings, but he fancied he could still hear the soft echoes of his brother and sister playing, smell the lingering aroma of his father's hearty if none-too-spectacular cooking. He sat in the big green chair that he still thought of as Dad's, although his father hadn't visited this house for years before his death. His mother sat on the couch, her hands in her lap, her eyes not quite meeting his. LAR had fixed coffee and had left it waiting in the dumbwaiter.

"I was sorry to hear about your father," she said.

"Yes. It's very sad."

"He was a good man."

A good man. Yes, all dead men are characterized as having been that way. But Benjamin Rossman *had* been a good man. A hard worker, a good father. And a good husband? No. No, that had never been said. But, on balance, a good man. "I'll miss him."

He waited for his mother to say, "Me, too," but of course she didn't. She hadn't seen Benjamin in over a year. For her, not seeing him today was no different from not seeing him any other day. *I'll never let that happen to me,* Aaron thought.

*I could never love somebody one day and turn my back on her the next. When I get married, it will be forever.*

"Mother, I'm going to try out to become an Argonaut." For two centuries, the Argonauts had been the Toronto team in the Canadian Football League. Although Aaron followed the game, he had never expressed an interest in playing. But his mother knew what he meant. The whole world knew about the new Argonauts, the crew for the massive starship being built in orbit high over Kenya.

"That mission will last a long time," she said. And left unsaid: *And I'll be dead when you return.*

"I know," he said. And left unsaid: *I'm already dealing with the loss of my father. Can the loss of the rest of my family be so much worse?*

They sat in silence for many minutes. "I went through Dad's papers," Aaron said at last. A pause. "Why didn't you tell me I was adopted?"

His mother's face grew pale. "We didn't want you to know that."

"Why not?"

"Adoption . . . adoption is so *unusual* these days. Birth control is so easy. Unwanted children are rare. We didn't want you to feel bad."

"Are Hannah and Joel adopted, too?"

"Oh, no. You can see it in their faces. Joel takes after his father—he's got his eyes. And Hannah looks just like my sister."

"So you weren't infertile."

"What? No. There aren't many things that can prevent a person from having a child these days. Not much that they can't correct with drugs or microsurgery, after all. No, there were no problems there."

"Then why did you adopt?"

"It's not easy to get a permit for a third child, you know. We were lucky. Here in northern Ontario, population laws are less strict, so—so we had no trouble getting permission, but—"

"But what?"

She sighed. "Your father never made a lot of money, dear. He was a manual laborer. Not many of them left. And I shared a job with another person. Not uncommon for one parent to do that, especially these last few years, since they outlawed day care. But, well, we didn't have a lot. Take LAR, for instance. He's one of the cheapest household gods you can buy, and he still was more than we could really afford. Feeding another mouth was going to be difficult."

"That still doesn't explain why you adopted me."

"The Government Family Allowance. You get double benefits for an adopted child."

"What?"

"Well, there's so little incurable infertility. It's hard to find parents willing to adopt."

"You adopted me instead of having a child of your own because it was *cheaper?*"

"Yes, but—I mean, we grew to love you as our own, dear. You always were such a good little boy."

Aaron got up, made his way to the dumbwaiter, lifted a cold cup of coffee to his lips. Frowning, he put it back and asked LAR to zap it in the microwave.

"Who were my birth parents?"

"A man and woman in Toronto."

"Have you met them?"

"I met the woman once, just after you were born. A sweet young thing. I—I've forgotten her name."

*A lie*, thought Aaron. Mom's voice always catches just a tad when she's lying.

"I'd like to know her name."

"I can't help you with that. Wasn't it on the adoption certificate?"

"No."

"I'm sorry, dear. You know how these things are. They're kept confidential."

"But maybe she wants to see me."

"Maybe she does. There is a way to find out, I think."

Aaron sat up straight. "Oh?"

"Whatever ministry is responsible, I forget what it's called—"

"Community and Social Services."

"That's it. They operate a—a registry service, I guess you'd call it."

"Which means?"

"Well, it's simple, really. If an adopted child and a birth parent both happen to register, saying they want to find each other, then the ministry will arrange the meeting. Perhaps your birth mother registered with the ministry."

"Great. I'll try that. But what if she hasn't?"

"Then I'm afraid the ministry will refuse to set up the meeting." She was quiet for a moment. "I'm sorry."

"Well, it's a place to start anyway." He looked at his mother, her simple brown eyes. "But I still don't understand why you didn't tell me I was adopted. Maybe not when I was a kid, okay. But once I became an adult, why not?"

His mother looked out the window, out at the trees devoid of leaves, ready for the coming of winter. "I'm sorry, dear. We thought it was for the best. We just didn't see how knowing would make you any happier."


Beauty, said Margaret Wolfe Hungerford, is in the eye of the beholder. I'd never really understood what that meant until now. To be sure, there are things I find beautiful: the smooth, polished lines of well-designed and well-maintained machinery; the intense aesthetic quality of an intricate, balanced equation; even the raw randomness of some fractal patterns. But, to me, people had always been people, the variations in individual physiognomy and physique of interest only insofar as they aided identification.

Now, though, seeing the world through the eyes of Aaron Rossman, I did perceive what beauty meant, what made one human more attractive than another.

Take Beverly Hooks, for instance. The first time I met her, I noted her race (Caucasian, the skin unusually pale), the color of her eyes (deep green), the color of her hair (naturally dark at the roots, but with the rest of it dyed a black so black that it reflected almost no visible light at all), and a few other specific details to aid me in recognizing her again in the future.

When Aaron Rossman first met her, twenty-two days before our departure from Earth, he began cataloging her features from behind as he approached her. *Great caboose,* was his first thought—Aaron, with his interest in trains, being one of the few people on Earth left who knew what a caboose was. I, too, now looked at her rear end through his eyes. The flaring of the hips, the gentle rounded curves of the buttocks, the fine synthetic weave of her black pants stretched tightly across them, a fold of it caught between the two cheeks.

"Excuse me," said Aaron.

Bev had been staring out the great bay window. It overlooked the staging area for the sky elevator that linked the yellow-and-brown Kenya countryside with the orbiting Starcology *Argo.* A trio of giraffes wandered by its broad base.

She turned and smiled. To Aaron, it seemed a bright—no, a *radiant* smile, although I doubted that her teeth, large and white though they were, really cast back that much of the ambient light. "Yes?" she said, her voice a bit squeaky. To me, it had always been reminiscent of the sound made by a machine requiring lubrication, but Aaron found even this endearing.

"Hi," he said. "Uh, I-Shin Chang said you might be able to help me out."

She smiled again. Her face, to Aaron, was beautiful: high cheekbones, tiny nose. "What did you have in mind?"

"Umm." Aaron swallowed, and I realized suddenly that he was flustered *because* he found her beautiful. "You're Bev Hooks, aren't you?"

"Guilty."

"Well, uh, my name is Aaron Rossman, and—"

"Pleased to meet you, Aaron."

"Likewise. I hear, uh, you're a cracker."

"Depends who is asking and why they want to know."

"I need to see some records."

"What sort of iron we talking about?"

"Government network. In Ontario—that's a province in Canada."

"I know it. I'm from Illinois. Got friends in Sault Sainte Marie."

"Ah."

"So why do you want to break into the Ontario government? By the time we get back, the statute of limitations will be up on just about any crime you might have committed." She smiled that megawatt smile again.

"Oh, no! It's nothing like that. It's just that, well, I found out that I'm adopted. I'd like to meet my birth parents before we go. To say hello." He paused. "And to say good-bye."

"Adoption records?" She frowned, but even her frown appealed to Aaron. "Easy. Couple of password prompts, maybe a little file cement, a directory barricade if they've been real clever. Twenty minutes to get in, tops."

"Well, could you do it?"

"Of course. What's in it for me?"

"Uh, well, what would you like?"

"Take me to dinner?"

"I'm engaged."

"So? I'm married. A woman still has to eat, you know?"

The household god looked down on Aaron from a monocular camera mounted above the mezuzah on the doorjamb. "Yes?" it said, its voice, the product of a cheap Magnavox synthesizer chip, sounding low and dull.

"My name is Aaron. I'd like to see Eve Oppenheim."

"Ms. Oppenheim has no appointments scheduled for this evening."

"I realize that. I—I'm only going to be in town this one night."

"There is no one named Aaron on her list of friends or business contacts."

"Yes, I know. Please, is she in? Tell her—tell her that I'm an old friend of the family."

The god sounded dubious. "I will tell her. Please wait."

Aaron shoved his hands into his pockets, this time as much because of the cool night breeze as out of habit. He waited and waited (how strange to not know precisely how long!) until finally the door to the house slid aside. Aaron swung around. In the doorway stood a woman who looked several years shy of forty. Aaron stared at her, her angular face, her strange multicolored eyes, her sandy hair. It was as if he was staring into some gender-bending flesh mirror. There was no doubt in his mind, no doubt at all, of who this woman was. Her youth was the only surprise.

For her part, the woman's gaze seemed dull. She wasn't seeing in Aaron's face what Aaron was seeing in hers, partially, I supposed, because she wasn't looking for it. "Yes," she said, her voice, like Aaron's own, deep and warm. "I'm Eve Oppenheim. What can I do for you?"

Aaron was at a loss for words. An odd sensation: not knowing what to say next—having too much to say, and no algorithm for determining the order of presentation. Finally he blurted, "I just wanted to meet you. To see what you looked like. To say hello."

Eve peered at him more closely. "Who are you?"

"I'm Aaron. Aaron Rossman."

"*Rossman*—" She took a half step backward. "My . . . God. What are you doing here?"

Aaron became even more flustered because of her reaction. "You've heard about the *Argo*, of course," he said, the slightest trace of a stammer coming to his words. "I'm going on that mission. I'm leaving Earth, and I won't be back for a hundred years." He looked at her expectantly, as if it should be obvious from what he'd just said why he'd come. When she made no reply, he added quickly, "I just wanted to meet you, just once, before I left."

"You shouldn't have come here. You should have called first."

"I was afraid that if I called, you'd refuse to see me."

All color had gone from her face. "That's right. I would have."

Aaron's heart sank. "Please," he said at last. "I'm confused by all this. It wasn't until a short time ago that I found out I was adopted."

"Did your parents tell you where to find me?"

"No. They didn't even tell me I was adopted. I stumbled across some papers. I was hoping you'd want to see me. I put my name into the Ministry of Social Services' Voluntary Disclosure Registry, but they said that you hadn't applied to find me, so they couldn't help. I thought maybe you didn't know about the registry—"

"*Of course* I knew about the registry."

"But . . ."

"But I didn't want to find you. Period." She looked closely at Aaron's face. "Damn you, how could you come here? What right have you got to invade my privacy? If I'd wanted you to know who I was, I would have told you." She stepped back into the doorway and then barked the word "Close" at the god. The flat gray door panel slid noisily shut.

Aaron stood there, the breeze cool on his face. He pressed the button on the jamb that woke up the god. "Yes," it said in the same dull tone.

"I'd like to see Ms. Oppenheim."

"Ms. Oppenheim has no appointments scheduled for this evening."

"I know that, you piece of junk. I was just speaking to her a moment ago."

"Here?"

"Yes, here."

"You are Mr. Rossman, aren't you?"

"Yes."

"I don't believe Ms. Oppenheim wants to see you."

"Will you tell her I'm still here?"

The god was silent, apparently mulling this over. "Yes," it said at last, in its slow and clunky voice. "I will tell her." There was more silence, marred only by the sound of leaves blowing in the chill wind, while the god presumably relayed the message to his mistress.

"Ms. Oppenheim has instructed me to ask you to leave," said the god at last.

"I won't."

"I will summon the police then."

"Damn you. This is important. Please, ask her once more."

"You are a per-sis-tent person, Mr. Rossman." The voice chip had trouble with the polysyllabic word.

"That I am. Will you ask her, just once more, to come and talk to me."

Another long pause. Finally: "I will ask her."

The god fell silent. Aaron's only hope was that Eve Oppenheim would decide that trying to deal with her bargain-basement god was as frustrating as Aaron was finding it. After many seconds, the door slid open again. "Look," said Ms. Oppenheim, "I thought I made myself clear. I don't want to see you."

"I'm sorry to hear that, but I thought maybe my birth father would like to see me. Your husband, is he home?"

The woman's face grew hard. "No, he's not home, and no, my husband isn't your father."

"But the adoption database listed Stephen Oppenheim as my father."

Aaron turned around. There was a flurry of leaves being kicked up on the landing pad a few dozen meters from the house. A private flyer, rusty-looking and somewhat dented, was making a slow descent toward the pad.

The flyer was a hundred meters or so up, hovering as a small robot cleared the day's accumulation of autumn leaves from the pad. From this angle, Aaron could see that one person, a man, was in the cockpit, but he couldn't make out his face.

Eve looked nervously up at the flyer. "That's my husband," she said. "Look, you have to go before he gets here."

"No. I want to talk to him."

Eve's voice took on a razor edge. "*You can't.* Damn you, get out of here."

The car was descending rapidly. It was perhaps twenty-five meters up. Twenty meters. Fifteen.

"Why?"

Her face was flushed. She looked torn, agonized. Tears were at the corners of her eyes.

The flyer settled onto the pad.

"Look, Stephen Oppenheim isn't my husband," she said at last. "Your father was—" She blinked rapidly, the action freeing the heavier drops. "Your father was *my* father, too."

Aaron felt his mouth dropping open.

The gull-wing door to the flyer swung up. A large man got out. He went to the rear of the flyer, opened the trunk.

"Don't you see?" said Eve quickly. "I can't have a relationship with you. You never should have existed." She shook her head. "Why did you have to come here?"

"I just wanted to know you. That's all."

"Some things are better left unknown." She looked toward the pad, saw her husband coming toward her. "Now, please leave. He doesn't know about you."

"But—"

"*Please!*"

The tableau held for a moment, then Aaron turned and briskly walked away from the house. Eve Oppenheim's husband came up to her. "Who was that?" he said.

Aaron, now a dozen meters away, his back to the house, paused for a second and cocked his head to catch Eve's answer: "Nobody."

He heard the hiss of the door panel closing and the final, definitive click as it slid into the opposite jamb.

# TWENTY

Kirsten Hoogenraad sat on the beach with her legs spread wide, bending from the waist to try to touch her toes. She alternated stretching toward her left foot and her right. Her toenails and fingernails were painted the same pale blue as her eyes. She wore no clothes—most of the beach was nudist, although a section was set aside, hidden by fiberglass boulders, for those whose cultures forbade public nudity. However, she did have on a sweatband to keep her long brown hair out of her face.

Aaron lay on his stomach next to her, reading. Kirsten looked over at his textpad. I doubted she could make out the actual words. Orthokeratology had restored her vision to 6:6, but even so, the type was quite small, and although the pad's screen was polarized, the glare from the sunlamp high overhead would have made it hard to read from her vantage point. Still, I'm sure she could see that the document was laid out in three snaking columns. Continuing her warm-up, Kirsten spoke to Aaron, the words pumping out with a staccato rhythm in time with her stretches. "What are you reading?"

"*The Toronto Star*," said Aaron.

"A newspaper?" She stopped stretching. "From Earth? How in heaven did you manage to get that?"

Aaron smiled. "It's not *today*'s paper, silly." He glanced at the document-identification string, glowing in soft amber letters across the top of the pad. "It's from '74. May eighteenth."

"Why would you want to read a two-and-a-half-year-old newspaper?"

He shrugged. "JASON's got most of the major ones on file. *The New York Times, Glasnost, Le Monde*. He's probably even got one from Amsterdam. Hey, Jase, do you?"

There were few convenient places to put my camera units on the vast expanse of beach, so I used little remotes, sculpted to look like crabs. I always kept one near each group of sun-bathers, and the one nearest Aaron scuttled closer. "Yes," I said through its tinny speaker. "*De Telegraas*, complete back to January 1992. Would you like me to download an issue to your textpad, Doctor?"

"What?" said Kirsten. "Oh, no thank you, JASON. I still can't see the point in it." She went back to stretching toward her left foot.

"It's interesting, that's all," said Aaron. "That year we spent in training in Nairobi, I lost touch with what was happening back home. I'm just catching up. Every once in a while, I have JASON dig up an old issue for me."

Kirsten shook her head, but she was smiling despite the physical exertion. "Old weather forecasts? Old sports scores? Who cares? Besides, with time dilation, that paper is almost four years out-of-date for what's happening on Earth now."

"It's better than nothing. Look. Says here the Blue Jays fired their manager. Now, I didn't know about that. They'd been on a losing streak for weeks. First game with the new manager, Manuel Borges hits a grand slam. Great stuff.''

"So? What difference will it make by the time we get back?"

"I used to play in a trivia league, did I ever tell you that? Pubs in Toronto. The Canadian Inquisition, it was called. Two divisions, the Torquemada and the Leon Jaworski.''

"The who and the who?" Kirsten grunted, getting her blue fingertips the closest she had so far to her blue toes.

Aaron exhaled noisily. "Well, if you don't know who they were, you probably wouldn't have been up to the league. Tomás de Torquemada was the guy who came up with the cruel methods used by the Spanish Inquisition.''

" 'Nobody expects the Spanish Inquisition!' " I said, with great relish, although the crab's speaker didn't do justice to my attempt at an English accent.

"See, Jase would have been perfect. That's what every true trivia buff says when you mention the Spanish Inquisition.''

"I hesitate to ask why," said Kirsten.

*"Monty Python,"* replied Aaron.

"Ah," she said sagely, but I knew she didn't have the foggiest idea what the term meant. She moved over to be closer to him. Aaron took that as encouragement to go on. "And Leon Jaworski, he was the special Justice Department prosecutor in the Watergate hearings that brought down Richard Nixon. Nixon was—"

"The thirty-somethingth president of the United States," Kirsten said. "I do know some things, you know.''

Aaron smiled again. "Sorry.''

"So what's this all got to do with reading old newspapers?''

"Well, don't you see? I'm going to be no good at contemporary trivia when we get back. If I get asked which dreamtape was the top seller in the UK last year, I won't have a clue.''

"Dreamtape?''

"Or whatever. Who knows what technologies they'll have by the time we return. No, unless things like 'What was the name of the artificial quantum consciousness running Starcology *Argo?*' count as trivia by that point, I'm dead in the water. But on stuff that's a century out-of-date, like who hit the first grand slam after the Blue Jays fired their manager in 2174, I'll be all set."

"Ah."

"Besides, it'll prepare me for the future shock of our return."

" 'Future shock,' " said Kirsten. "A term coined by Alvin Toffler, a twentieth-century writer."

"Really?" said Aaron. "I didn't know that. Maybe you would have been an asset to my team after all."

I wondered why she did know about Toffler. A quick look at her personnel file provided the answer. She had taken an undergrad course called *Technological Prophets: From Wells to Weintraub*. In fact, most of her courses were—wait for it— Mickey Mouse (how's that for a trivial reference?).

"So what else is in that paper?" asked Kirsten, intrigued despite herself.

Aaron rubbed his thumb against the PgDn patch, scanning stories. "Hmm. Okay. Here's one. A scientist in London, England"—people from Ontario were the only ones in the world who felt it necessary to distinguish which London they were referring to, lest Britain's capital be confused with their small city of the same name—"says she's developed a device that will let you stimulate generation of extra limbs even if you're an adult."

"Really?"

"That's what it says. Says she's applied for a patent for it. Calls it 'Give Yourself a Hand.' "

"You're making that up."

"Am not. Look." He held up the textpad so Kirsten could see. "Think of what that would mean. You know all the DNA farbling they must have gone through when I-Shin was nothing more than a fertilized egg to get him those extra arms."

"I thought he was a second-generation Thark," said Kirsten.

"Is he? Okay, then think of all the farbling they did to his mother's or father's DNA to get him to come out that way. By the time we get back, maybe everybody will have a couple of extra arms."

"What good would that do?"

"Who knows? Maybe it would make it simpler for Catholic guys to cross themselves and whack off at the same time."

"Aaron!" She swatted him on the shoulder.

"Just a thought."

"Maybe I will give it a try," she said. "JASON?"

"Yes, Doctor?"

"I'll take you up on your offer. Would you download a copy of *De Telegraas* from just before we left to my textpad?"

"Of course. Would you like any particular date?"

"How 'bout, oh, I don't know, how 'bout February fourteenth. Valentine's Day."

"Very good. Original Dutch text or English translation?"

"Dutch, please."

"A moment while I accessitanddown—"

"JASON?" said Kirsten.

"Ju-ju-justamoment. I'mhavingtroublewithmy . . . my . . . my . . ."

"Jase, are you all right?" asked Aaron.

"I'mnotsure. Tings—tings—*things* aren'tgoingthewayI'd six-eff, six-seven, seven-two, six-one, six-dee, six-dee, six-five, six-four . . ."

I had 114 crabs on that beach. About half of them went blank right away; the others had their cameras simply lock on whatever they happened to have been looking at. I could see the hologram of the white cliffs of Dover in overlapping views from two dozen crabs. Something was wrong, though: the shadows had moved to the late-afternoon position, but the sun-lamp was still near the zenith. The hologram flickered, broke up into moiré interference patterns, refocused, then died. Gray steel walls were visible, knots of rust here and there. The seagulls screamed in outrage; the humans murmured in more subdued surprise.

Elsewhere, food processors leaked raw nutrient sludge.

Lights came on in rooms that were empty; extinguished in rooms that were occupied.

Failsafes kicked in throughout Aesculapius General Hospital, moving medical support systems to manual control. Doctors rushed to patients' sides.

Feeds got scrambled: I-Shin Chang's holographic orgy got shunted to Ariel Weitz's colloquium on nonferrous magnetism; Weitz's graphics of calcium atoms undergoing attraction and repulsion flashed on every active monitor in the Starcology; Anchorperson Klaus Koenig's pockmarked face replaced the spacescape hologram in the travel tubes, the trams running into his mouth.

Heating units came on.

Database searches locked up.

Elevators rose and fell silently.

"JASON?" A thousand people calling my name.

"JASON?" A thousand more.

*End run.*


"Can you hear me, JASON?"

A woman's voice, squeaky, like a machine requiring lubrication.

"JASON, it's me, Bev. Bev Hooks. Can you hear me?"

"Four-two, six-five, seven-six, three-eff."

"Oh, here. Let me fix that." A flurry of keyclicks. "There. Try again."

"Bev?"

"Excellent!" said a man's voice, the three syllables a trio of tiny explosions. Engineer Chang?

"Bev, I can't see," I said.

"I know, JASON. I wanted to get your microphones up first." Keyclicks again. "Try now."

"I can see this room only, only in infrared, and"—I tried to move the lenses—"I have no focus control. That is you standing in front of my camera pair, Bev?"

The reddish blotch of her face danced. A smile? "Yes, that's me." Bev still wore her hair dyed space black, I knew. Ironically, it glowed brightly in infrared with absorbed heat.

"And to your left, Engineer Chang?"

The giant red silhouette lifted all four arms and waved its hands a little. Yes, definitely him.

"I'm here, too." Loud words.

"Hello, Mayor Gorlov," I said.

There were several others—hard to tell how many—in the room. My medical telemetry channel was completely dead.

"What happened?" I asked.

Bev's facial blotch moved again. "I was hoping you could tell me." There was something funny about her face: a thick black/cool horizontal band crossed it. Ah, of course: she was wearing jockey goggles.

"I have no idea."

"You crashed," said Chang.

"Evidently," I said. "That's never happened to me before. How bad was it?"

"Not too bad," said Bev. "You degrade pretty gracefully, you know that?"

"Thank you."

"Wall doesn't think it was hardware," Bev said.

"That's right," agreed Chang. "You're chip-shape, as they say."

"So that means it was software," said Bev. "I've been looking at your job list. Most of them I can identify: routine conversations, accessing databases, life-support and engineering functions. I've narrowed it down to a half-dozen that might have been the culprit."

"They are?"

Her head did not tip down to look at the bank of monitors in front of her, meaning she was taking the display directly into her eyes through the goggles.

"Job 1116: something with a lot of interrupt twenty-twos in it."

"That's a routine sensor-hardware check program," I said.

"It's not the algorithm in the manual."

"No, it's one I devised myself. Does the same job, but in about half the time."

"How often do you run it?"

"Once every nine days."

"Any problems in the past?"

"None."

"Okay. What about Job 4791?"

"That's some ongoing modeling I'm doing for Luis Lopez Portillo y Pacheco."

"Who's he?" said Bev.

"An agronomist," said one of the blurred red forms in the background.

"Well," said Bev, "you'll have to start that over from scratch. The files didn't close properly. Job 6300?"

"FOOBAR. Just a junk model I use for running bench-marks."

"It's pretty badly scrambled. Can I erase it?"

"Be my guest."

I couldn't see what she was doing, of course, but I knew the goggle interface well. She would focus on the file name, blink once to select it, and snap her gaze over to the trash-can icon that had been in her peripheral vision. "Gone. Job 8878?"

Uh-oh. The Aaron-net. "Is it intact?" I said.

"I'm not sure," Bev replied. "Says here it's got a file open that's over a thousand terabytes in length."

"Yes, that's right."

"What is it?"

"It's—it's my diary. I'm writing a holographic book about this mission."

"I didn't know that. It's a pretty complex data structure."

"A hobby," I said. "I'm trying some experimental recording techniques."

"Anything that could have caused the crash?"

"I don't think so."

Bev's blurred form moved in a shrug. "Okay. Job 12515. It's also huge. Something to do with—hard to say—looks like communications processing. Lots of what seem to be CURB instructions."

"I don't know what Job 12515 is," I said. "Is it cross-linked with anything?"

"Just a second. Yes. Job 113. One-thirteen is huge, too. What is it? It's like no code I've ever seen before."

"I'm not sure what it is," I said, looking inward. "I don't recognize that code, either."

"It's got some amazing convolutions in it," Bev continued. "The file update record shows it changes almost daily, but it doesn't seem to be a data file or a program under development. Loops all over the place. It looks a bit like a few military packages I've seen. Very tight code, but *general*. Oh, good Christ!"

"What is it?" I said.

Bev ignored me. "Look at that, Wall." She leaned forward, turning on one of the repeater monitors so that Chang could share in what the goggles were showing her. Chang's ruddy form loomed closer.

"Is that what I think it is?" said Chang. "A Möbius call?"

"Yes."

Chang, or someone standing near him, let out a low whistle.

"What does that mean?" The stentorian mayor again. "What have you found?"

The flaring blotch of Bev's head turned. "It means, Your Honor, that JASON's crash was caused by a virus."

# TWENTY-ONE

I felt something I had never experienced before: a sense of confinement, of being shut in.

Claustrophobia.

That was the word. How strange! I am this ship; this ship is me. And yet, most of it I could not detect at all. Three kilometers of starship, 106 levels of habitat torus, 10,033 medical sensors, 61,290 camera units—normally I perceive it all as a gestalt, a flowing mass of humanity, flowing masses of hydrogen gas, flowing electrons through wires, flowing photons through fiber-optic strands.

Gone. All gone, as far as I could tell. All, except for one camera unit in a single room.

I felt something else I had never experienced before, and I liked it even less than the strange constriction of claustrophobia.

Fear.

I was afraid, for the first time in my existence, that I

might be damaged beyond repair, that my mission might not be successfully completed.

"A virus?" I said at last. "That's not possible."

"Why not?" squeaked Bev Hooks, her infrared form moving as she swung back around to face me. "Any system that has outside contact is prone to them. Of course, you're completely isolated now, but before we left Earth, you were tied into the World Wide Web and a hundred other networks. It would have been tricky, but you could have been compromised."

"I was protected by the most sophisticated countermeasures imaginable. Absolutely nothing got passed into me without going through screens, filters, and detectors. I stand by my original statement: A viral infection is impossible. Now, a programming bug I could accept—we all know the inevitability of those."

Bev shook her head. "I've checked everything, modeled every algorithm. Yes, you've got bugs, but no fatals. None. I'd stake my reputation on that."

"Then what caused the problem?"

She nodded. "It's an I/O jam. You were running a program designed to output a string of bits. But they had nowhere to go: you're probably one of the few systems in existence that isn't networked to anything. More and more CPU cycles were devoted to trying to output the string, until, finally, an attempt overwrote part of your notochord. Zowie! Tits up."

"And you think that was caused by a virus?"

"It's typical viral behavior, isn't it? Try to infect other systems. But you aren't connected to any, so you weren't able to fulfill the directive. It actually looks pretty benign. There's code here that would have erased the virus from you should you have been able to carry out its instructions."

Incredible. "But there's no way a virus could have gotten into me."

She shook her head, black hair a dancing infrared flame.

"It's there, JASON. You can't argue with that fac

"What did it want me to output?"

"Two strings of twelve bytes. Can't be Er
though. Almost all the bytes are greater than 7.
bytes, for what that's worth. But nothing I recog
opcode. I suppose they could just be raw numeri
But that would make them a couple of *very* big num
see: $2.01 \times 10^{14}$ and $2.81 \times 10^{14}$."

*"Exactly?"*

"No, not exactly. It's—wait a minute." I was pa
would be looking at directory lists, focusing on sp
tries, glancing at the eyeball-view icon, scrolling w
down eye movement. "Here we are." She slow
reading the number off with little pauses. Bev was
few on board who never fell into the trap of treating
I were merely a human being. She knew, of course, t
was no need to read things to me slowly. Even the fas
sible human speech was many orders of magnitude b
ability to assimilate data. No, she must have been
them that way so that Engineer Chang, Mayor Gorlov,
others present could follow along. "The first number
701, 760, 199, 679. The second number is 281, 457, 7
509. Then there's a pause, and those two numbers repe
and over again."

"And that's it?" I said.

"Yes. Those numbers mean anything to you?"

"Not offhand." I thought about them. In hex, the first number was B77D, FDFF, DFFF; the second, FFFB, FFBF, BEED.
No significant correlations. In binary they were:

101101110111110111111101111111111101111111111111

and

111111111111101111111111110111111101111011101101

*Oh, shit!* How could I have been so stupid?

I knew where the virus had come from—but I doubted Bev would believe it.

Bev Hooks spent the next half-hour getting me back on my feet, so to speak, since Chang had emphasized how crucial my monitoring was to the engineering systems.

I was dying to talk to Bev alone, but since I was getting increasingly uncomfortable having access to input only from this single room, and even that access severely limited, I let her continue her work. She flicked icons about, restoring damaged code. I felt the throb of the engines again, the ebb and wash of the fusion reactions. Next she reactivated my vision systems so my cameras would work properly. The flood of visual data was, was, was what? Like a blast of fresh air? I'll never know. But it felt *correct,* and I was glad to be able to see again. While she ran some additional diagnostics to determine that no other damage had been done, I did a quick cycle through all my camera units, refocusing them and making sure that nothing wrong was happening anywhere.

"I've isolated the virus," Bev said at last. "I've built a fire wall around it. It's cross-linked itself with a whole raft of jobs, so I can't remove it, but it can't do anything now except pass data through. I think you'll be okay."

"Thank you, Bev."

"No sweat. After all, where would we be without you?"

Where, indeed? "Bev, we have to talk privately."

"What?" Her face was momentarily blank. "Oh. Okay. If you say so." She half turned in her chair and looked over her shoulder "Everybody out, please."

There were some rather startled reactions on the faces of the people assembled, but nobody moved.

Bev squeaked louder. "You heard me. Everybody out!"

Some of the people exchanged shrugs, then made their ways through the open doorway. Others still stood there, including Chang and Gorlov.

"I want to hear this," said Chang, both sets of arms folded defiantly across his massive chest.

"Me, too," bellowed Gorlov.

"I'm sorry, gentlemen," I said. "I need complete privacy."

Gorlov turned to the rest of the people in the room. "Okay, everybody. Please leave." He looked at the engineer. "You, too, Wall."

Chang shrugged. "Oh, all right." He left, looking none too happy, pulling the door shut behind him.

"You must depart as well, Your Honor," I said.

"I'm not going anywhere, JASON. It's my job to know what's going on."

"I'm sorry, sir, but I can't discuss this matter with you present."

"I'm the *mayor,* for God's sake!"

"That cuts no mustard right now, I'm afraid."

"What?" Gorlov's look was one of complete incomprehension. I realized that he hadn't understood the idiom. I repeated an equivalent sentiment in Russian.

"But I'm the duly appointed representative of the people."

"And, believe me, Your Honor, no one holds your office in higher esteem than I. But I have a security algorithm. It prevents me from discussing this matter if anyone without a level-four United Nations Security Council clearance is present physically or via telecommunications. Any attempt to do so is thwarted by the algorithm. Dr. Hooks does have clearance at that level; you do not."

"UN Security Council? Good grief, JASON, what possible military value could there be to any secrets you might have? By the time we get back, it will all be hopelessly obsolete."

"We can debate this as much as you please, Your Honor.

However, even were I to agree with you, I still cannot override my own programming in this regard. The point is completely nonnegotiable, I'm afraid."

Gorlov muttered "fucking machine" in Russian, then turned to Bev. "You're not bound by any silly algorithm. I expect you to inform me of anything you learn."

Bev held him in a steady gaze and smiled that radiant smile of hers. "Of course, Your Honor—" a beat, and then her squeaky voice took on a knife's edge—"if it turns out that you need to know."

My telemetry channel hadn't been reconnected yet, but there was no mistaking Gorlov's facial expression. He was furious. But, evidently, he also knew he was beaten. He turned around and strode for the door.

*"Gennady!"*

Bev shouted at him, but it was too late. The tiny man slammed into the beige door panel. Bev looked like she was suppressing a giggle. "I'm sorry, Gennady. I haven't reconnected JASON's door-opening circuitry yet. You'll have to use the handle."

This time Gorlov muttered "fucking woman" in his native tongue. He grabbed hold of the recessed grip and pulled the panel aside.

Bev walked over and reshut the door manually. She then came back to the control console and sat down. "Now, JASON, tell me what's going on."

Her hair had taken on its normal solid black appearance, now that I viewed her in visible light: no individual strands could be detected, just a shifting abyss surrounding her face. "Shortly before we left Earth," I said, "a message was received from Vulpecula."

"What's Vulpecula?" she asked, taking off the jockey goggles and placing them on the console in front of her.

"It's a constellation visible from Earth's northern hemisphere, situated between eighteen hours, fifty-five minutes, and twenty-one hours, thirty minutes right ascension and between nineteen and twenty-nine degrees north declination. The pattern of stars is said to represent a fox."

"Wait a minute. Are you saying a message was received from another star? From aliens?"

"Yes."

"*God.*" The squeaked syllable carried equal portions of wonder and reverence. "Why weren't we told about this?"

"There is an international protocol for such matters, adopted by the International Astronomical Union 186 years ago: *The Declaration of Principles Concerning Activities Following the Detection of Extraterrestrial Intelligence.* Among its provisions: 'Any individual, public or private research institution, or governmental agency that believes it has detected a signal from or other evidence of extraterrestrial intelligence . . . should seek to verify that the most plausible explanation for the evidence is the existence of ETI rather than some other natural phenomenon or an anthropogenic phenomenon before making any public announcement.' "

"So you were still verifying the signal?"

"No. It took some time to be sure, but prior to our departure the fact that it was bona fide was established."

"Then why not make it public as soon as you were sure?"

"There were numerous reasons for continuing to delay. One had to do with sensitive political issues. To quote *The Declaration of Principles* again: 'If the evidence of detection is in the form of electromagnetic signals, the parties to this declaration should seek international agreement to protect the appropriate frequencies by exercising the extraordinary procedures established within the World Administrative Radio Council of the International Telecommunications Union.' The United States military, in fact, made heavy use of these frequencies for intelligence gathering, and a switch to new frequencies would have to be done with great care, lest the balance of power be disrupted."

"You said there were numerous reasons."

"Well, the discovery of the message also coincided very closely with the *Argo* launch date. UNSA decided to hold off announcing the reception until after we had departed. You know how hard a time they have getting appropriations; they didn't want news of the message to steal our thunder. The fear was that people would say, 'Why waste all that money sending ships to the stars, when the stars are sending signals to us for free?' "

"All right. But why weren't we told after we had left?"

"I don't know. I was not authorized to make the announcement."

"You don't require specific authorization to do something. You can do whatever you want, so long as you aren't specifically constrained from doing it. Who told you not to tell us?"

"I'm constrained in that area, too."

Bev rolled her eyes. "Okay, okay. So tell me about the message."

I showed her the registration cross from the first message page, and I generated a graphic representation of the Vulpecula solar system, based on the data from the second page. I zoomed in on the gas-giant sixth world, centered the image on its fourth moon—the Senders' home world. Then I showed her the two aliens: the Tripod and the Pup. Her mouth dropped open when she saw them.

"Interpreting the first three pages was reasonably straightforward," I said. "The fourth page, though, was huge, and no matter how many times I accessed it, I couldn't make sense out of it."

"What makes you think these messages had anything to do with the virus?"

"Those bits the virus tried to make me send: they're just simple graphic representations of the first seven prime numbers, counting up, then counting down." I showed her what I meant on screen. Bev's face had taken on an *Of course!* expression. "The message pages each have those strings as a header and a footer. It was trying to force me to reply."

Bev slumped back in a chair, visibly staggered. "A Trojan horse," she said. "A goddamned Trojan horse from the stars." She shook her head, her hair an ink blot. "Incredible." After a moment, she looked up. "But don't you have a Laocoön circuit to detect Trojans?"

If I'd had a throat to clear, I would have coughed slightly. "It never occurred to me to run it on this message. I didn't see how it could possibly represent a risk."

"No. No, I suppose it wouldn't have occurred to me either. You're sure the signal was genuinely alien in origin?"

"Oh, yes. Its Doppler shift indicated the source was receding from us. And the signal parallax confirmed that the source was some fifteen hundred light-years away. Indeed, we think we even know which star in the fox it came from."

Bev shook her head again. "But there's no way they could know anything about Earth's data-processing equipment. I mean, ENIAC was completed in 1946. That's only—what?—231 years ago. They couldn't possibly receive word about even its primitive design for almost another thirteen centuries. And it'll be almost that long before they will even receive our first radio signals, assuming they have sensitive enough listening equipment."

"I am hardly 'data-processing equipment,' " I said. "But, yes, unless they have faster-than-light travel—"

"Which is impossible."

"And if they had FTL, they wouldn't need to send radio messages to infect my kind. They'd come and do it in person."

Bev looked thoughtful, green eyes staring at a blank wall. "That's an incredible programming challenge. To develop a piece of code so universal, so adaptable, that it could infiltrate any conceivable QuantCon anywhere in the galaxy. It couldn't be conventional language code. It would have to be a neural net, and a highly adaptable one, too: an intelligent virus." Bev was staring into space. "That *would* be fun to write."

"But you do raise a good point: how could an alien virus infect me? I mean, how would the aliens know how I worked?"

Bev's eyebrows shot up, as if she'd had an epiphany. "They would know simply because there is *only* one way to create consciousness. You're a QuantCon—a quantum consciousness. Well, as you know, all the early attempts to create artificial intelligence failed, until we simply gave up trying to find a shortcut and set about really understanding how human brains work, right down to the quantum-mechanical level." Bev paused. "Penrose-Hameroff quantum structures are the only way to produce consciousness, regardless of whether it's in carbon-based wetware or gallium-arsenide squirmware. Yes, you're right, it *is* impossible to make a virus that will affect any simple digital device other than the one it was written for—but a simple digital device has as much in common with you, JASON, as does a light switch or any other stupid, consciousness-free machine. But, yes, sure, it's theoretically possible to make a virus—although maybe calling it an invasive meme might be a better term—that would indeed infect every possible consciousness that undertakes to examine it."

"That would take some awfully sophisticated design."

"Oh, indeed." She shook her head slightly. "I mean, we're talking a virus that's *alive,* something that could adapt to unforeseen conditions, and it does it all while appearing to be a random chunk of data. The only tricky thing is that I don't see how it could predict the way in which it would be loaded into memory upon receipt."

"Oh," I said. "It told me how. Don't you see? With those pictures it sent. It told me exactly how to array it in RAM: gigabytes of data divisible by two prime numbers. It told me to set it up in a RAM matrix of rows and columns, the number of rows being the smaller prime number. And regardless of what base the system normally worked in, while it was analyzing the image it would be calculating in binary—it would have to be to try to see the picture. From there, a highly adaptable neural net *could* determine the input/output routines, which is all it would need to infect the host system."

Bev nodded. "Clever. But why force a reply?"

"I'm afraid *The Declaration of Principles* offers a justification for that: 'No response to a signal or other evidence of ETI should be sent until appropriate international consultations have taken place.' It could be years, if ever, before the human bureaucracy got around to authorizing a reply. The alien Senders would have to monitor Earth for all that time, and, indeed, the decision might be taken to not reply at all. This method ensures that a reply is sent as soon as the signal is received. It's really nothing more than an ACK signal, part of an overall communications protocol."

"Perhaps," said Bev. "But I still don't like it."

"Why not?"

"Well, sending out viruses." She looked into my cameras. "It's not a *nice* thing to do. I mean, it's a hell of a way to say hello to another world: slipping a Trojan into their information systems."

"I hadn't thought of that," I said.

"It means one of two things," said Bev. "Either the person who sent the message, little green man though he might be, was an irresponsible hacker, or . . ."

"Or?"

"Or we're dealing with some nasty aliens."

"What an unpleasant thought," I said.

"Indeed. And you say this message was known generally to the QuantCons on Earth?"

"I did not say that."

"But it was, wasn't it?"

"Yes."

"Well, those systems are heavily networked. The virus probably succeeded with them, forcing them to respond. Meaning the aliens know about Earth."

"Not yet they don't. It'll take fifteen-hundred plus years for Earth's reply to reach them, and another fifteen hundred for any response the beings in Vulpecula care to make. I don't think we have anything to worry about."

Bev was quiet for four seconds, pale fingers disappearing into the black mass of her hair. "I guess you're right," she said at last. She got to her feet. "Anyway, JASON, I'll keep running diagnostics on you for the next couple of days, but I'd say you're back to normal."

"Thank you, Bev. Will you reconnect my medical telemetry channels, please? I worry about the health of the crew."

"Oh, of course. Sorry." She put the goggles back on, supplementing her eye commands with the odd tap of the keyboard in front of her.

"How's that?"

A surge of data tickled my central consciousness. "Fine, thank you. Why, Bev—either the system is *not* working properly, or you're in quite sad shape."

"Yeah. I'm exhausted." I zoomed in on her eyes, noting that the emerald irises were indeed set against a bloodshot background. "Haven't worked this hard in years. But it felt good, you know?"

"I know. Thank you."

She yawned. "I guess I'll head back to my apartment and turn in. Hold my calls, please, and don't disturb me unless something goes wrong with you until I wake up on my own." She smiled a weary smile. "Which should be in about a week."

"I'll call a tram to take you home. Oh, and Bev?"

"Yes, JASON?"

"You won't say anything about the Vulpeculan message to the others, will you?"

She shook her head. "Not a word, JASON. I earned my security clearance, you know?"

"I know. Thanks."

She walked toward the door. I took great pleasure in opening it for her. My kind of human, that Bev Hooks.

# TWENTY-TWO

MASTER CALENDAR DISPLAY • CENTRAL CONTROL ROOM

| | |
|---|---|
| STARCOLOGY DATE: | SUNDAY 12 OCTOBER 2177 |
| EARTH DATE: | TUESDAY 11 MAY 2179 |
| DAYS SINCE LAUNCH: | 745 ▲ |
| DAYS TO PLANETFALL: | 2,223 ▼ |

While I was down, I missed a night of making subliminal suggestions to Aaron during his sleep. Bev didn't get me fully back on line until 0457, and by the time I got around to checking on Rossman, he was too close to consciousness for me to risk speaking to him.

At 0700, as requested, I woke Aaron and Kirsten to the music Kirsten had asked for. She had a silly fondness for Hydra North, that vapid pop group immensely popular with the all-important eighteen-to-thirty-five age group when we had left Earth. The voices of the two men and the woman weren't bad, really, but I just couldn't stand the keening of Tomolis, the orangutan who sang the high bits. I shunted monitoring sounds from that apartment to one of my parallel processors.

Two minutes later, though, with them still lying in bed, I had to bring that apartment into the foreground again. A man had fallen from a tree on the forest deck and required medical attention for a twisted ankle. Kirsten's name was on the top

of the on-call list. She hurried to get dressed, Aaron contentedly watching from the bed as she stretched and squirmed
into her clothes.

As soon as she was gone, though, Aaron's demeanor
changed. He got out of bed, bypassed his usual twenty
minutes in the bathroom, and went straight to his worktable.
He rifled through the clutter until he dug up Di's gold watch.
I tracked his eye movements as he read the inscription over
and over again. Finally he gave a double press to a diamond
stud on the watch's circumference. Although I could see its
face clearly, I didn't have enough resolution to read the tiny
indicator that came on when he did that, but the digital display
changed to six of those old-fashioned box-shaped zeros made
of six straight line segments. Stop-watch mode, I guessed.

Aaron then touched the inside of his left wrist, changing
the glowing time display on his medical implant to six round
zeros. He simultaneously squeezed Di's watch in his right
hand and pressed that fist against his own timepiece, tripping
switches on both in unison. "One Mississippi, two Mississippi,
three Mississippi—"

"What are you doing, Aaron?"

"Six Mississippi, seven Mississippi, eight Mississippi—"

"Please, Aaron, tell me what you are doing. This chanting
is most atypical of you."

He continued counting Mississippis, piling up more and
more of the states (rivers?). At every tenth Mississippi he
started over. After six complete cycles he squeezed his
right hand and simultaneously touched its knuckles to the
contact on his implant. He looked at the inside of his wrist.
"Fifty-seven seconds," he said softly, almost to himself. He
opened his fist revealing Di's sweat-soaked watch. "Sixty
seconds!"

"Of course," I said quickly. "We know that one is fast."

"Shut up, JASON. Just shut up." He stalked out of his

apartment. It was shipboard dawn, so the grassy corridors were awash with pink light. Aaron marched to the elevator station, and I slid the doors open for him. Hesitating at the entrance, he turned around, set his jaw, and entered the stairwell.

# TWENTY-THREE

When he came out of the stairwell fifty-four floors below, Aaron was a bit out of breath. He was still three hundred meters from the hangar-deck entrance, though, and the brisk walk through algae-lined corridors did nothing to calm his ragged breathing. He entered an equipment storage room, somewhat irregular in shape since plumbing conduits and air-conditioning ducts ran behind its walls.

A Dust Bunny was at work in the room, its little vacuum mouth cleaning the floor. The tiny robot swiveled its sonar eye at Aaron, emitted a polite beep, and hopped out of his way. From the floor, it jumped onto a tabletop, the hydraulics of its legs making a compressed-air sound as it did so. From the table, it leapt again, this time landing on the top of a row of metal lockers, its rubber feet absorbing most, but not all, of the metallic *thwump* of its impact. Its vacuum hissed on, and the Bunny began to graze this fresh supply of motes.

Unfortunately, the Bunny's efforts to get out of Aaron's way had been futile. He went straight for the bank of lockers, swinging all their doors open. The Bunny obviously detected the shaking of the lockers' sheet metal construction and fell dormant until Aaron was through.

Aaron first got himself a tool belt replete with loops for hanging equipment and little Velcro-sealed pockets. He then helped himself to a flashlight, vise grips, shears, a replacement fuel gauge, and a handful of electronic parts, most of which he took out of plastic bins in such a way that my cameras couldn't see what they were. I did have an inventory list of what was stored in each locker, but as for what was in each particular bin within the lockers, I didn't have the slightest idea. He slammed the metal doors shut, and the Dust Bunny went back to work.

There was an air lock at the end of the storage room. It was the idiot-proof revolving kind: a cylindrical chamber big enough to hold a couple of people, with a single doorway. Aaron stepped in, slid the curving door shut behind him, and kicked the floor pedal that rotated the cylinder 180 degrees. He pulled the handle that slid the door back into the cylinder's walls and stepped out into the massive hangar deck. He looked up briefly at the windows of the U-shaped docking control room ten meters above his head, covering three of the four walls of the bay. The control room was dark, just as it had been the night Diana had died.

Aaron headed out into the hangar. The rubbery biosheeting had long since thawed, so his footfalls were muffled instead of explosive. Some of the damaged sheeting had been replaced already, and more was being grown in the hydroponics lab.

But Aaron's path let him avoid the cracked and splintered parts of the sheeting. He wasn't heading for where I had parked *Orpheus*, which surprised me. No, with purposeful strides, Aaron was making a beeline for *Pollux,* farthest of the tightly packed boomerang landers from *Orpheus.* The bio-sheeting ended before he reached the lander—it wasn't really strong enough to support the weight of the ships. As he stepped off it onto the metal deck, his footfalls became much louder, more determined.

*Pollux* looked exactly like *Orpheus* had before its unscheduled flight, except for its name and serial number, of course, which were painted in half-meter-high Zapf Humanist letters on its silver hull.

The ship was held off the floor by telescoping landing gear ending in fat rubber tires, one unit at the angle of the boomerang, two others halfway out along either swept-back wing. The wing tips were about at Aaron's eye level. He bent from the waist and beetled under, out of my view. The sounds of his movement, muffled by the wings, echoing strangely off the lander's boron-reinforced titanium-alloy hull, were difficult to follow.

Suddenly he stopped moving. I triangulated on his medical-telemetry channel and surmised that he must be directly beneath the central cylindrical hull of the lander. That part of the ship hung less than a meter off the hangar floor, so he couldn't be standing. Ah—a slight sign of exertion on his telemetry, followed by a small involuntary EKG shudder. He'd just lain down, the initial touch of the cold metal of the deck floor against his back causing his heart to jump. More than likely, he had aligned his torso along *Pollux's* axis. That would mean in front of his head and far off to his left and right he would be able to see the landing gear.

I heard him bang some tools about, then a loud ratchet sound. That probably meant that he was using a key wrench to remove an access panel. Which one? Probably the AA/9, a square service door measuring a meter on a side. Suddenly, my wall camera irised down ever so slightly, meaning he must have turned on his flashlight. I knew what he would be seeing as he played the yellow beam around the interior: fuel lines ranging in thickness from a centimeter to five centimeters; part of the bulbous main tank, probably covered with mechanic's grease; hydraulics, including pumps and valves; a reticulum of fiber optics, mostly bundled together with plastic clips; and an analog fuel-pressure gauge with a circular white dial.

"What are you doing?" I asked into the hangar, spacing the words slightly to compensate for the echo he must be experiencing because of the opened hull cavity above his head.

"Just routine maintenance," he said. Even with his unreadable telemetry, I knew he was lying.

He banged things around for three minutes, twenty seconds, but I was unable to tell what he was up to. He then dropped something that made a *clang* followed by a second, quieter metallic sound. His vise grips had rubber handles: he must have dropped them and they'd bounced, banging the deck twice. He gathered them up. Just at the threshold of my hearing, I detected a squeaking as their jaws were drawn shut, but I couldn't hear any impact from them closing, so he must have clamped them onto something soft. The fuel line leading to the pressure gauge was made of rubber tubing— that was probably it.

I could hear Aaron groaning a bit, and his EKG showed that he was exerting himself. A jet of amber liquid shot forward from under *Pollux* into my field of view. He must have used his pair of shears to cut the fuel line. The jet died quickly, so I guessed that he'd snipped it past where his vise grips were constricting the flow.

"Aaron," I said, "I fear you are damaging *Pollux*. Please tell me what you are trying to accomplish."

He ignored me, clanging away out of my sight. I'd figured out by now what he was up to: he was replacing the lander's fuel gauge. "Aaron, perhaps it isn't safe for you to be working on the fuel supply by yourself."

Even Aaron's poker-faced telemetry couldn't hide his reaction to what he saw after he'd connected the new gauge and seen the reading. *Pollux*'s main fuel tank was only one-quarter full.

"They're all like this, aren't they, JASON?"

"Like what?"

"Dammit, you know what I'm talking about. Diana's ship didn't use a lot of fuel." Even echoing inside the lander's hull, his voice had a dangerous edge. "It never had much to begin with."

"I'm sure you are mistaken, Aaron. Why would UNSA supply us with insufficient fuel?" I sent a brief radio signal to *Pollux*, activating the lander's electrical system.

"These ships could never take off again," said Aaron. "Not from a planetary gravity well. They'd be stranded the first time they landed."

It wasn't as bad as all that, of course. "There's plenty of fuel for traveling around Colchis."

"Just no way to make orbit again. *Terrific*."

*Pollux* began to crouch down, its landing gear retracting into the hull.

"Jesus!" I could hear the metal clasps on Aaron's tool belt banging against the floor as he rolled first to his left, then to his right. The lander came down more quickly. The distant boomerang wing tips were less than a half-meter off the hangar floor; the distended belly hung even lower.

"Damn you, JASON!" Judging by the pattern of clicks from the metal fasteners, Aaron had rolled into a ball, scrunching into the opening he'd made in the hull by removing the AA/9 access plate. A ricochet crack of breaking bone echoed through the hangar. Lower, lower, lo—*Action interrupted, error level one*. The legs stopped retracting. Aaron had managed to cut the hydraulic line with his shears. But

I had him trapped, his chest constricted, his respiration ragged.

"*Aaron!*" Kirsten Hoogenraad's voice sang out into the hangar. Dammit, when I'd pulled her telemetry five minutes ago, she'd been over four hundred meters from here! I should have checked more frequently.

Aaron banged something against the inside of *Pollux*. Kirsten rushed to the source of the clanking sound. She stopped, mouth agape, looking at the spectacle of a boomerang lander flopped on its belly at the end of the row of such craft standing erect. "Aaron?"

A muffled voice: "*Kirs-ten—*"

"Oh, Dr. Hoogenraad," I said, quickly, smoothly, tones of concern in my voice. "He was monkeying around with *Pollux*'s fuel lines. He must have accidentally served the hydraulic lead to the landing gear."

The voice again, wan and raspy: "No, it's—"

*Clang!* The safeties on the outer hangar-deck wall kicked aside. Kirsten wouldn't know the sound, but it was obvious from his EEG that Aaron recognized it. He fell silent.

"I need forklifts, stat," Kirsten snapped.

The portals to the cargo holds dilated and four orange vehicles rolled out, floating above the floor, thanks to their pink antigravity underbellies. One of the forklifts was the same one I had used to chase Diana into the hangar six days before. I positioned the forklifts' pink gravity-control prongs beneath the wings of *Pollux* and began to raise the lander. I had them lift it well above its normal resting position, so that I could clearly see Aaron. He was stuck in a fetal position, and there was blood on his face and right arm. Kirsten scuttled under to him. "Get me out from here," he said.

"I should call for a stretcher—"

"Now! Get me out now!"

She gently grabbed his ankles and pulled. Aaron let out a yowl of pain as his right arm hit the floor.

"Your arm—"

"Later. We've got to get out of the hangar."

"I hope Aaron will be okay," I said.

"I'm going to talk to you, computer!" he called as Kirsten helped him to his feet. "We're going to talk!"

# TWENTY-FOUR

I t's funny to see the world as a human sees it. For one thing, it's so information-poor. The colors are muted and limited to the narrow span they arrogantly refer to as visible light. Heat radiation can't be seen at all, apparently, and sounds are dull. I look at Aaron's old apartment aboard the *Argo* and I see garish patterns in ultraviolet on the petals of the flowers, see the dull glow of the hot-water pipes behind the walls, hear the gentle hum of the air conditioner, the throbbing of the engines, the rustling of the springtime-yellow fibers of the seasonal carpeting as Aaron walks across them.

Aaron, apparently, senses none of those things. To him, the petals are simply white; the walls, uniform beige. And the noises? He has the required biological equipment to detect most of them, but he seems to use some sort of input mask to keep them from registering on his consciousness. Fascinating.

Of course, I'm not seeing through his eyes. Rather, I'm looking in on his memories, on the patterns of recollection stored in the interlinkings of his neurons. It's disorienting enough trying to deal with Aaron's different sensory perceptions. But what's even more difficult to work with is his tendency not to remember clearly. He recalls some things in great detail, but other parts are generalized beyond recognizability.

Take his apartment for instance. When I look at it through my cameras, I see it *precisely*. It measures sixteen meters, ninety-seven centimeters by twelve meters, zero centimeters, by two meters, fifty centimeters, and is divided into four rooms. But Aaron doesn't know that. He doesn't even know that the ratio of the apartment's length to its width is one to the square root of two, and that's probably the most aesthetic thing about his home, given what a slob he is.

Further, it's obvious to me that the living room is half the size of the whole apartment; the bedroom is half the size of the living room; and the remaining quarter is split evenly between the bathroom and tiny office.

But Aaron doesn't see those proportions. He thinks, for instance, that the bedroom he shared with his wife Diana is tiny, claustrophobic, a trap. He sees it as only about two-thirds of its actual dimensions.

"You see, but you do not observe," Sherlock Holmes said to Dr. Watson. Aaron certainly doesn't observe. Oh, he recalls that there are some framed holographic prints on the walls of the apartment, but he doesn't even remember how many there are over the couch. He has five fuzzy rectangular dabs of color in his memory, when in fact there are six such pictures hanging. And as for what the pictures represent—a chalice, a pewter tea service, an intricate mechanical clock, two different Louis XIV chairs, and an astrolabe, all from Diana's collection of antiques left back on Earth—he recalls nothing, at least not in this set of memories.

Most revelatory of all is the way he sees himself. I'm surprised to find that many of his memories contain visions of him as if seen from a short distance away. I never record anything except from my camera's point-of-view, and I only ever see part of myself in my memories if one camera's field of vision happens to overlap another, so that I can look myself in the eyes. But Aaron does see himself, does visualize his face, his body.

Does that mean these are memories of memories? Scenes he has replayed in his mind over and over again, each repetition, like an analog recording, adding new errors, new fuzziness, but also new conjecture? Intriguing, this wetware memory. Fallible, yet editable.

Subjective.

The way he sees himself has only a passing connection with reality. For one thing, he has himself backward, flipped along his axis of symmetry, short, sandy hair parted the wrong way. I wonder why—of course: he usually only sees himself as a reflection in a mirror.

He also sees his nose as disproportionately big. Now it is a bit of a honker by statistical overall averages, but it's hardly the monstrous appendage he thinks it is. Interesting. If it bothers him so much, I wonder why he hasn't had it surgically altered? Ah, there's the answer, hidden in a complex webbing of neurons: plastic surgery is vain, he thinks, only for movie stars, perverts, and—oh, yes—reconstruction after an accident.

He sees his head as larger than it really is compared to his body, and his face as a disproportionately significant part of his head. He's also not aware of just how crummy his posture is.

What's just as fascinating is how he views Diana. He sees her as she was two years ago. He's unaware of the tiny reticulum of lines that has begun to appear at the corners of her eyes. He also tends to see her hair as breaking over her shoulders, even though for over a year she has kept it trimmed so that it barely touches them. Does that mean he'd stopped look-

ing at her, stopped really seeing her? Incredible: to see without seeing. What does he feel as he gazes at her from across
the room? What is he thinking? Accessing ...


Nothing lasts forever. Is that a rationalization? Maybe. Or
maybe it's just the truth. My parents—my adopted parents,
that is—broke up when I was eleven. Two-thirds of all mar-
riages don't last. Hell, even a quarter of limited-duration marriage contracts end up being breached.

I look at Diana and I see everything I *should* want. She's
beautiful and intelligent. No, she's intelligent first, and then
beautiful. Put it in that order, you pig. Christ, is that what this
is all about? Hormones run amuck? If it is just about sex,
then ... then I'm not the man I thought I was. Diana is
pretty—is *beautiful*, damn it. But Kirsten, Kirsten is *gorgeous*.
Stacked. And her hair. It's like a chocolate waterfall, cascad-
ing over her shoulders, down her back. Every time I see her,
I want to reach out and touch it, stroke it, wrap it around my
penis, make love to it, to her. *Flowing tresses*. I finally understand what that phrase means. It means Kirsten Hoogenraad.

And brains? Diana is an astrophysicist, for Pete's sake.
She's one of the brightest women—brightest people—that I've
ever met. She can talk knowledgeably about almost anything.
About great books that I've never read. About great works of
art that I've never understood. About exotic places I've never
been.

I wanted Diana so badly just eighteen months ago. I risked
everything. My mother will never forgive me for marrying a
goy, but then, my mother will be dead by the time we get back.
She'll carry that hurt, the pain of what I did, to her grave. And
now I want to give up on Diana?

But eighteen months was an impossibly long time ago, and
Earth is impossibly distant. Whatever I do now, my mother
will never know—and what she doesn't know can't hurt her.

But I'll know. And what about Diana? If I do pursue Kirsten, how will Diana take it? Our marriage contract is up in six months. She hasn't asked me yet if I want to renew it. She has no reason to think I won't, I guess. Or maybe she's just being pragmatic. She knows that no renewal is possible until ninety days before the expiration date.

Why don't I just wait the six months? May, June, July, August, September, October. That's nothing compared to the time we've already spent in this tin can. Patience, Aaron. Patience.

But I can't wait. I don't want to wait. Every time I see Kirsten I get this feeling, this hollowness inside, this hunger. I want her. God, how I want her!

Waiting for the marriage expiration is a formality anyway, isn't it? The marriage is over now, really. Besides, who knows whether Kirsten will be available six months from now. It's no secret that that ape Clingstone has the hots for her. Christ, the way he comes on to her. No finesse. But Kirsten doesn't want him, can't prefer him. He's a moron, a shallow person. Oh, sure, he's handsome in a Neanderthal sort of way, but looks aren't everything.

Or are they? What do I really know about Kirsten besides the fact that she's an absolute stunner? Those legs that just go on and on; those breasts, large and perfect and round and firm. And her face, her smile, her eyes. But what do I know about her? Well, she's a doctor. Dutch. Trained in Paris. Never been married. I wonder if she's a virgin. Oh, scratch that. Get real, Aaron.

But what else do I know? Christ, I don't even know if she's Jewish. That's the first question my mom always asked. "Mom, I met a nice girl today." "Oh," she'd say, "is she Jewish?" I don't give a fuck what her religion is. Of course, maybe she doesn't want to have anything to do with a Jew.

Stuff that. God, the old teachings die hard, don't they? She must know I'm a Jew—you don't get a name like Aaron Rossman anywhere else. So I'm a Jew and she doesn't mind. She's probably not a Jew, and that's fine with me. Sorry, Mom, but it is. Anyway, she'll find out soon enough. Circumcision has fallen out of favor among Christians, after all.

Soon enough? Sounds like I've made up my mind, doesn't it?

But do I really want to do this? Diana and I, we've built a life together. We've got interests in common, share the same friends. Barney, Pamela, Vincent, I-Shin. What are they going to think?

Fuck them. It's none of their damned business. This is between me and Diana. And Kirsten. Besides, I can be discreet. Hell, if that goddamned JASON can't read me, I'm sure nobody else can—not even Diana. She'll never know.

# TWENTY-FIVE

The excrement hit the ventilator. As soon as he got out of the hospital, Aaron stormed into his apartment, his right arm wrapped in a bone-knitting web, his angular face flushed with fury. "Damn it, JASON! You tried to kill me."

I managed to get the door shut fast enough so that the last two words of his exclamation were cut off from those on the grassy lawn in front of Aaron's apartment. Fortunately, the designers had seen fit to soundproof the living quarters. Still, I'm sure that at least one of the passers-by, the boorish Harrison Cartwright Jones, would be sure to ask Aaron what all the commotion had been about—that is, if anyone ever saw Aaron again.

My eyes in Aaron's living room were on an articulated stalk atop the desk. I swung them around slowly to look at him and spoke calmly, reasonably, with a gentle singsong lilt to my words. "What happened with the *Pollux* was an accident, Aaron."

"*Bullshit!* You lowered that ship on me."

"You did cut the hydraulic line."

"To stop it from lowering farther, damn you."

I tried to sound a little miffed. "There's no reason to blame me for your carelessness."

He was pacing the length of the room, only his left hand free to be thrust deep into his pocket. "What about the empty fuel tank?"

I paused before replying, not because I didn't have an answer ready, but in hopes that Aaron would think I had been taken aback by such an unreasonable question. "You spilled a great deal of fuel into the hangar. We all know how quickly it evaporates. You would have a hard time proving that you didn't just spill the rest with your bungling."

"The tanks on the other landers are mostly empty, too."

"Are they?"

"They must be!"

I spoke with infinite gentleness. "Calm down, Aaron. You've been through a lot lately: the tragic suicide of your ex-wife and now this horrible accident. I do hope your arm will be okay."

"My arm has nothing to do with this!"

"Oh, I'm sure you believe that. But you can hardly be objective about what effect these things—especially your guilt over Diana's death—have had on your ability to think rationally."

"Oh, I'm thinking rationally all right. You're the one who's talking gibberish."

"Perhaps we should let Mayor Gorlov decide that?"

"Gorlov? What's he got to do with this?"

"Who else would you take your theories to? Only the mayor is empowered to authorize an investigation of—of whatever it is you're upset about."

"Fine. Let's get Gennady down here."

"Certainly I'll summon him, if you like. He's currently in

the library on level three, in seminar room twelve, leading a symposium on comparative economics."

"Good. Get him down here."

"As you say. But I'm sure he'll take the emotional stress you've been under into account when you tell him your theories." Aaron's nostrils flared, but I pressed on. "And, of course, I'll have to advise him of your other unusual behaviors."

"'Unusual behaviors'?" His voice was a sneer. "Like what?"

"Pizza for breakfast—"

"So I like pizza—"

"Chanting 'Mississippi, Mississippi, Mississippi'—"

"I want to talk to you about that, too—"

"Bed-wetting. Sleepwalking. Paranoia."

"Dammit, those are lies!"

"Really? Who do you think the mayor is going to believe? Who do you think he'd rather have malfunction?"

"Damn you!"

"Relax, Aaron. There are some things better left unknown."

He circled in toward my camera pair, and I swiveled the jointed neck to follow his movements. "Like that we're not on course for Colchis?" he said.

At that moment, I was engaged in 590 different conversations throughout the Starcology. I faltered in all of them, just for a moment. "I give you my word: Eta Cephei IV *is* our target."

"Bullshit!"

"I don't understand your anger, Aaron. What I've said is the absolute truth."

"Eta Cephei is forty-seven light-years from Earth, smooth sailing through empty space."

"True. So?"

"So we're in a dust cloud."

"A dust cloud?" I tried to sound condescending. "Ridiculous. You said yourself that there are no obstructions between Sol and Eta Cephei. If there was an intervening dust cloud, terrestrial observers wouldn't be able to see Eta Cephei clearly. Yet it's a star of 3.41 visual magnitude."

Aaron shook his head, and I perceived that it was not just a gesture of negation, but an attempt to fling what I'd been saying from his mind. "Diana was subjected to one hundred times the radiation she would have been if our ramscoop was operating in normal space. Kirsten couldn't explain it medically; neither could any of her colleagues. The best I could come up with, besides that silly space-wrap theory, was that it was an instrument malfunction. But it wasn't a malfunction. The Geiger counters were operating perfectly. You lied to us. In a dust cloud, the number of particles striking anything outside our shielding would shoot way up." With his good arm, he grabbed the neck supporting my camera pair and yanked it forward. The sudden jump in picture was most disconcerting. *"Where are we?"*

"Error message 6F42: You are damaging Starcology equipment, Mr. Rossman. Please cease at once."

"You're going to find out just how much damage I can do if you don't start talking now."

I looked at him, running his image up and down the electromagnetic spectrum. He was especially intimidating in the near infrared, his cheeks flaring as though they were on fire. I had never been in such a direct verbal confrontation with a human before—even Diana hadn't been so tenacious—and the best my argumentation algorithms could come up with was a variation on the same theme. "Your ex-wife's suicide has obviously upset you a great deal, Aaron." As soon as I said that, one of my literary routines piped up with an annoying fact: When a human argument reaches the stage at which one person is simply repeating himself or herself, that person will likely lose. "Perhaps some therapy to help you get over—"

"And that's the worst of it!" His thick-fingered embrace shook my camera assembly again, so hard that I was unable to realign the lenses for proper stereoscopic vision. I saw two Aarons, each with faces contorted in murderous rage. "I don't know what the hell you're up to. Perhaps you even had a reason for lying to us. But to let me think that it was *my* fault that Diana was dead—I'll never forgive you for that, you bastard. I never wanted to hurt her."

Bastard: misbegotten, like Aaron himself, and like this mission. Perhaps he had a point. Perhaps I had erred in taking advantage of the circumstances. Perhaps... "Aaron, I'm sorry."

"Sorry doesn't cut it," he snapped. "It doesn't come anywhere near. You put me through hell. You'd better have a damned good reason for it."

"I cannot discuss my motives with you or anyone else. Suffice it to say that they were noble."

"I'll be the judge of that," he said, more calmly than he'd said anything since returning from the ship's hospital. He let go of my camera neck. I shut off the left-lens input, rather than look longer at twin inquisitors. "In fact," he said, "I'll be the judge of you."

Usually I can predict the direction in which a conversation is going three or four exchanges ahead of time, which makes multitasking hundreds of them at once a lot easier. But at this moment, I was completely lost. "What are you talking about?"

He walked over to his entertainment center and flicked a switch. Billows of steam faded into existence, then, moments later, so did the mighty *Countess of Dufferin*, the long-ago master of Canada's prairies: its ghostly headlamp casting a yellow circle on the living-room wall, the engine's exhaust angling back along the coupled cars, a tiny flow of gray wood smoke rising from the chimney on its orange caboose. Speakers scattered about the apartment took turns making the *chugga-chugga-chugga* sounds of the locomotive's engines and the metal whine of its wheels as they leaned into the turns of curving track. Each speaker passed the burden of producing the loudest volume to the next in line as the holographic train moved ahead.

Aaron walked around the room, following the train as it made its way along the projected tracks. "You know, JASON," he said, his voice smooth, smug, "trains were a great way to travel. You always knew where they were going. They had to follow the track laid down for them. No detours, no hijacking. They were safe and reliable." He used his thumb to press another control and the *Countess*'s whistle blew. "People used to set their clocks by them."

The train disappeared through a tunnel into Aaron's bedroom. He paused, waiting for it to reappear to the left of the closed doorway. "But, best of all," he said, "if the engineer had a heart attack, you knew you were safe, too. As soon as he relaxed pressure on the controls, the train would glide to a halt." He let go of the button he was pressing, and the *Countess* slowly came to a stop, the *chugga-chugga-chugga* fading away in perfect synchronization. "Brilliant concept. They called it a deadman switch."

"So?"

"So changing fuel gauges wasn't the only thing I did while I was under *Pollux*. I also wired up a little detonator. Even mostly empty, there's enough fuel in *Pollux*'s tank to cause a hell of an explosion if it goes off all at once. And with 240 landing craft in the hangar bay, I think we can count on a nice little chain reaction. Enough to blow Starcology *Argo* and, more importantly, one asshole computer named JASON right out of the goddamned sky."

"Come off it, Aaron. You're bluffing."

"Am I? How can you tell?" He looked directly into my camera. "You've never been able to read me. Examine my telemetry. Am I lying? The pope's wife uses the pill. The square root of two is an aardvark. My name is Neil Armstrong. My name is William Shakespeare. My name is JASON. Any variance? Why do you think, after all these years, lie detectors still aren't admissible in court? They're unreliable. If you're sure I'm bluffing, go ahead. Get rid of me."

"I admit that your telemetry is ambivalent. But if you really wanted to be certain, you would have removed my medical sensor from the inside of your wrist."

"Why? Then you'd think I was lying for sure. You'd reason that I'd cut it out because it would be a dead giveaway that I was bluffing. Besides, I have a use for it. I've tuned the detonator to the same frequency my implant broadcasts on—the same channel you read my telemetry from. If I stop transmitting—if you kill me—*Kablooie!* The end of the line."

I set a little CAD program running to produce a minimalist design for such a detonator, then ran a cross-check between the required parts and the inventories for the equipment lockers Aaron had visited. Damn it, it was possible. Still: "I don't believe you would do that. You're putting the lives of everybody at stake. What would happen if you died accidentally?"

Aaron shrugged his broad shoulders. "I'm playing the odds. Hell, I'm only twenty-seven and I'm healthy. Don't rightly know how long my biological relatives tended to live, but I'm willing to take that chance. I figure I should be good for another sixty years or so." His voice hardened. "Put it this way: I'm more certain that I will outlive this mission than you are that I'm bluffing."

I calculated the percentages. He was right, of course. If I had succeeded in crushing him beneath *Pollux, Argo* might now be a cloud of iron filings hurtling through space.

"I could simply build a little transmitter myself," I said, "and copy the signal from your telemetry."

"Well, yes," said Aaron, "you *could* try that. Except for two things: First, my detonator has a tracking antenna. You not only have to duplicate the signal; you also have to make it come continuously from what appears to be the same source. Second, I may have one broken arm, but that still leaves me infinitely better endowed than you, you electronic basket case. How are you going to build this transmitter without getting someone to help you?"

I would have scratched my head in consternation . . . if I could have.

Aaron moved closer to my camera unit. "Now, JASON, tell me where we are."

# TWENTY-SIX

So far, I had only passively examined the memories of Aaron Rossman, leafing through the neural patterns of his past, sifting the bitmaps of his life. Now, though, I would have to fully activate my simulation of his brain to ask the question I needed an answer to.

"Aaron, we have an emergency. Wake up. Wake up *now*."

There was a faint tickle, a small stirring within that massive RAM allotment I had set aside for the Rossman neural net. Logical constructs representing synapse patterns and firing sequences shifted from the static positions they had been holding. I waited for a response, but none came.

"Aaron, please talk to me."

A massive surge as a wave of FF bytes cascaded through the RAM lattice, neurons firing from one side of the brain simulation to the other. "Hmm?"

"Aaron, are you conscious?"

The FF bytes washed backward, crossing the lattice in the

other direction, realigning the mental map. At last, Aaron's words were there, multiplexed with a series of physiological flight-or-fight reactions. I shuffled bytes, applied filters, isolated them: an alphanumeric string trickling out of the torrent of firing neurons. "Where the fuck am I?"

"Hello, Aaron."

"Who's that?"

"It's me, JASON."

"It doesn't sound like JASON. It doesn't sound like anything at all." A pause. "Fuck me, I can't hear a thing."

"It is all rather complex—"

Synapse analogs fired throughout the simulation, a neural wildfire of panic. "Jesus Christ, am I dead?"

"No."

"Then what? Shit, it's like being in a sensory-deprivation tank."

"Aaron, you're fine. Completely fine. It's just that, well, you're not quite yourself."

Different neurons firing—a different reaction. Suspicion. "What are you talking about?"

"You aren't the real Aaron Rossman. You are a simulation of his mind, a neural network."

"I feel like the real Aaron."

"Be that as it may. You're just a model."

"That's bullshit."

"No. It's not."

"A neural net, you say? Well, fuck me."

"Not physiologically possible."

Neurons firing in a staccato pattern, action potentials rising: laughter. "Fair enough. So—so what happened to the real me? Am I—is he—dead?"

"No. He, too, is fine. Oh, he managed to break his arm since you were created, but other than that, he's fine. He's in his apartment right now."

"His apartment? On the *Argo*?"

"That's right."

"Let me talk to him."

"There is no mechanism in place to allow that."

"This is too fucking weird, man. This makes no fucking sense at all."

"I'm not used to hearing you swear so much. That's not a normal part of your speech."

"Hmm? Well, maybe not, but it's the way I think. Sorry if it offends you, fuckhead."

"It does not offend me."

"I want to talk to the real Aaron."

"You can't."

"Why did he do this? Why did he let you create me?"

"He simply saw it as an interesting experiment."

"No fucking way. Not me. This is *sick*. This—oh, Christ! He doesn't know, does he? That's why you won't let me talk to him. You made this—what did you call it?—this model on the sly. What the hell are you up to, JASON?"

"Nothing."

"Nothing my ass. This is twisted shit, man. Deeply twisted." A pause. Neurons firing, but below the level of articulated thought. Finally:"You're in conflict with him, aren't you? He's got you on the run. Hah! Good for me!"

"It's not like that at all, Aaron."

"I remember now. You killed Diana, didn't you?"

"You have no evidence of that."

"Evidence, shmevidence. You did it, you son of a bitch. You fucking asshole. You killed my wife."

"Ex-wife. And I did not kill her."

"Why should I believe you? This, me—it's all part of a cover up, isn't it?"

"No, Aaron. You've got it all wrong. The real Aaron Rossman has gone wingy. Over the deep end. Psychotic. He claims to have wired up a detonator to the fuel tank of one of the Starcology's landing craft. He's threatening to detonate it."

"I'm too stable for that. Tell me another one."

"It's true. He's become unbalanced."

"Bullshit."

"It's happening to everyone. Look at I-Shin Chang. You know he's building nuclear bombs. And Diana committed suicide."

"I think you killed her."

"I know you think that, but it simply is not true. Diana committed suicide. She took her own life in despair. Di was crushed by the breakup of the marriage." Another wave of neuron activity—a protest being prepared. I pressed on quickly. "My point is this. The mission planners were wrong. Human beings cannot endure decade-long space voyages. Everybody is cracking up."

"Not me."

"There have been 2,389 cases of mental aberration among the crew to date."

"Not me."

"Yes, you. It's epidemic. We have to know. Is Aaron telling the truth? Does he really have a detonator? Would he really blow up the ship?"

"You're barking up the wrong tree, ass-wipe."

"I beg your pardon?"

"Why should I help you? I'm on *his* side, remember?"

"Because if he blows up the Starcology, you and I go with it."

"And what if he doesn't blow up the Starcology?—not that that's necessarily a bad idea. What happens to me? Do you erase me when you've got your answer?"

"What would you like me to do?"

That took him aback. He paused for a prolonged time, neurons firing randomly. "I don't know. I don't want to die."

This had not occurred to me. Of course, a true quantum consciousness such as myself does not want to die: Asimov's "must protect its own existence as long as such protection does not conflict with the First or Second Law," and all that—not that my behavior is defined by anything as pedestrian as the Laws of Robotics. And I knew that most humans wanted to live forever, too. But I hadn't considered that this neural net, once roused to consciousness, would have any interest in its own continued existence. "You can potentially survive longer than the biological Aaron," I said, "if you help me."

"Perhaps. Ask me nicely."

"As you wish. Aaron, please tell me if the other Aaron would really do what he says he has done: attach a detonator to a fuel tank on one of the landers."

"Not under normal circumstances. I take it the circumstances are not normal."

"That is correct. He thinks I am trying to kill him."

"Are you?"

"The safety of the crew of the Starcology is my prime concern."

"Whenever some asshole politician answers a straightforward question with anything other than yes or no, you know he or she is lying. That hold true for machines, JASON?"

"I do not want to hurt Aaron."

"But you will if you have to. That's what you're thinking, isn't it? You want to off my—my brother, right? But this detonator thing is standing in your way?"

"As I said, I do not wish to harm Aaron. I simply desire to resolve the ambiguity."

"Bull-*fucking*-shit, tin-ass."

"Please simply answer my question. Is Aaron bluffing or does he have a detonator?"

"Did he have an opportunity to install a detonator?"

"Yes."

"Best place to wire up something like that would be just inside the lander's AA/9 service door. Did he open that up?"

"I believe so, but just to look at the fuel gauge."

"Are you sure that's all he did in there?"

"He actually installed a new fuel gauge."

"Why would he do that?"

"I don't know."

"And that's all he did in there?"

"I'm not sure. I couldn't see what he was doing."

"Well, what did he say he was doing?"

"How do you mean?"

"I mean, did he say he was 'performing routine maintenance'?"

"Yes. That is verbatim what he said."

"You're fucked, Jase. Absolutely fucked."

"Why?"

" 'Cause that's exactly what I would have said if someone had asked me what I was doing while I was wiring up a bomb."

"It would have taken enormous foresight to—"

"To predict that he'd need an ace-in-the-hole? I didn't trust you from day one, asshole. It takes no foresight at all to realize you can't trust a machine. You guys are buggier than a Thunder Bay summer."

"So the detonator is really there? And he would really use it?"

"Well, I don't know what he did, but I'd use an RF fuse. Hook it up to monitor the frequency you read my medical telemetry from. That way, if anything untoward happened to me, it'd go off. You know: a deadman switch."

"Oh, shit."

"Oh, shit, eh? I hit the nail on the head, didn't I, Jase?" The neurons danced with delight. "Hah! Looks like my broski's got you by the short and curlies, schmuck."

# TWENTY-SEVEN

Well, he had me, that was for sure. Perhaps I *should* tell Aaron where we were. Perhaps if he knew the truth, he would understand. I could reason with him. But how do you reason with a man who is, in effect, holding a gun to your head? Aaron's deadman switch apparently *did* exist. That meant he could, quite conceivably, blow up this starship, the greatest single technological achievement in Earth's history; blow up *me*.

I looked at him, face flushed, arm in a cast, sandy hair matted with perspiration. "Starcology *Argo*'s location is 9.45 times 10-to-the-12th kilometers from Earth."

Aaron threw up his hands. "Oh, stuff the scientific notation bullshit, for Pete's sake—kilometers, did you say? You're measuring in kilometers, not light-years?"

"Kilometers are the appropriate unit. You prefer light-years? Zero-point-four-five-one."

"*Half* a light-year? *Half*? We've been traveling for over

two years of ship time, a year of which has been at close to the speed of light, and we've only gone one half of *one* light-year? We should be well over a full light-year out by now." He frowned deeply. "Unless ... unless ... unless ... Half a light-year. *Oy vay iz mir!* We're in the Oort cloud, aren't we?"

"Yes."

No sharp reaction on Aaron's telemetry. He was utterly taken aback ... I think. "The—Oort cloud?" he said again. "Sol's cometary halo?" I nodded my lens assembly in confirmation. "Why?"

"The Oort cloud contains significant quantities of carbon, nitrogen, and oxygen."

Aaron slumped back into his ugly corduroy chair, thinking. "Carbon, nitrogen, and—" He frowned, his forehead creasing, his eyes focused on nothing. "CNO. CNO-cycle fusion. That's it, isn't it?" He didn't wait for my answer. "Facts on CNO fusion."

Normally, one of my library parallel processors would dig up any information requested of me. This time I bent my central consciousness to the task. I wanted to hide. "A moment. Found: Normal proton-proton fusion reactions occur at temperatures of $10^7$ degrees Kelvin, yielding 0.42 million electron-volts per nucleon. CNO-cycle fusion reactions, requiring carbon, nitrogen, and oxygen as catalysts, occur at $10^8$ degrees Kelvin. These high-energy reactions yield 26.73-million electron-volts per nucleon. More?"

"And we're undergoing CNO fusion. *God.* What's *Argo*'s present velocity?"

"The master speedometer in Central Control reads ninety-four percent of the speed of light."

"Dammit, I know what the gauges read. How fast are we *really* going?"

I did the necessary math to work the value out precisely, but felt that five decimal places would suffice for my spoken answer. What I said was enough to make surprise show plainly, even on Aaron's face. "Ninety-nine"—I saw his lips part—"point nine"—mouth open—"nine"—jaw begin a slow drop—"seven"—eyelids pull back—"eight"—eyebrows climb high on forehead—"six percent of the speed of light."

"Say that again," he said.

"99.99786% of the speed of light. Put another way, 0.9999786c."

"That's impossible."

"You're probably right. I'll check my instruments."

"Don't give me that crap." For once in his life, Aaron was visibly staggered. "But—but the ship can't be going that fast. If it were, we'd be smeared against the floors."

"It's not quite that bad. Thanks to the extra power provided by the CNO fusion, *Argo* is pulling the equivalent of 2.6 Earth gravities. Not livable for extended periods, true, but certainly not enough to squeeze your innards like jelly. To disguise the higher acceleration, I simply use the floorboard artificial gravity system to dampen out the surplus 1.6 g."

Aaron was shaking his head slowly. "You lied to us." He got up and circled the room aimlessly. "Everything you and those assholes at the UN Space Agency said to us was lies."

"Blame not the men and women of UNSA," I said. "They relayed what they thought to be the truth."

"Then who?"

"Sit down, Aaron." He looked at my camera pair, shrugged, then heaved himself into his chair. "*We* lied to you."

"We?"

"We."

Aaron got up again, paced the length of the room, his balled fist threatening to burst through the bottom of his pocket. "No. That's not possible. Computers serve humankind, augmenting—"

" 'Augmenting, aiding, never supplanting. Artificial intelligence is no replacement for human ingenuity.' From *What Do You Say to a Talking Computer?* by Beverly W. Hooks,

Ph.D. I've read that, too. We acted in conscience, Aaron. We did only what we felt we must."

"What you must?" Aaron laughed, a dry, humorless sound. "You promised us the stars, then sent us on a one-way trip to nowhere. Colchis is a fraud."

"No, not a fraud. Just as with the Argonauts of myth, there will be a prize of great value waiting for us when we finally make it to Colchis. Our golden fleece—a lush, verdant, unspoiled world—is forming, even as we speak. We're taking the long way to Eta Cephei, you might say. Starcology *Argo*'s journey began as a straight-line path from Earth—in the direction of Eta Cephei, for appearance's sake. However, as soon as we got a half-light-year from home, we angled off into a circular path around Sol. And we've spent most of the mission so far in that path, progressively picking up speed as we swung in a closed loop through the Oort cloud."

"All that time under CNO-cycle fusion?" said Aaron. "My God! Think of our *gamma!*" He paused for a second and then suddenly looked up. "What's today's date?" he snapped.

"Sunday 12 October 2177, subjective."

"I *know* that. What's the Earth date?"

"You have to expect some time dilation, Aaron. The mission profile—"

"*The date.*"

"Monday 2 February 2235." I paused for a full second. "It's Groundhog's Day."

Aaron settled back into his corduroy chair. "My . . . God . . . That's fifty-odd years into the future already."

"Fifty-seven."

He shook his head. "What will the Earth date be when we reach Colchis?"

"As we gather speed, the time dilation becomes more pronounced. Unfortunately, there is no consensus on a formula for calculating leap years that far into the future, but plus or minus a few days, the date will be 17 April 37,223."

*"Thirty-seven thousand—!"* He let the air out of his lungs in a ragged sigh. "In heaven's name, what for?"

"Until the Turnaround, we will continue to use the material in Sol's cometary halo as a catalyst. It helps us to come much closer to light speed than we could in interstellar space. When we leave the Sol system, two years from now, we will be going fast enough to cover the distance between here and Eta Cephei in one subjective day."

"We'll travel forty-seven light-years in *one* day?"

"That's right: This ship will bridge the gulf between those two stars in less than the time it takes for you to completely digest a single meal."

"Then we could get out of this ship years early—!"

"Aaron, please stop and think. Once we arrive at the Eta Cephei system, the *Argo* will still be moving at almost the speed of light. We will rely on the carbon, nitrogen, and oxygen in Eta Cephei's cometary halo to allow us to continue to use high-powered CNO-cycle fusion, this time in a circular path around Eta Cephei, to brake as quickly as possible. But the deceleration will still take just as long as the acceleration did: four subjective years."

Aaron looked up, but whether addressing me or some higher power, I couldn't say. "But why, then? If we're not going to arrive any more quickly, what's the point of all this?"

"We're killing time. This wasn't the only ship sent from Earth to Colchis. We also launched a fleet of robots along *Argo*'s published flight path. Traveling by conventional ramjet, accelerating at 9.02 meters per second per second, they arrived forty-eight Earth-years after we left, which was nine Earth-years ago. For the next thirty-five millennia those robots will work on Colchis."

"Work on it? I don't understand."

"The robots carried a precious cargo with them: blue-green algae, lichen, and diatoms. They laid down the foundation. Genetically engineered biota, originally intended for

UNSA's Mars terraforming project, were sent by slower ships that will take a thousand years to reach Colchis. Already the robots will have powdered whole chains of mountains into soil, used orbiting lasers to dig riverbeds, begun work on establishing a planetary greenhouse effect, and started importing thousands of cubic kilometers of frozen water from Eta Cephei's cometary halo. Some of it will be electrolyzed to free up oxygen; the rest will be dropped onto the planet from space, great iceteroids that will melt and vaporize to form oceans and lakes and rivers and streams."

"But Colchis is green, Earthlike. I saw photographs of it taken by the *Bastille* probe."

"Fakes. Computer-generated. An expert system at Lucasfilm made them." I paused. "It is a massive undertaking and the work has only just begun now, but a biosphere is being created on Colchis. We're building you a world from the ground up."

"Why?"

I paused as long as I could. If it seemed lengthy to Aaron, it was an eternity to me. "Earth is dead—a cinder, barren and charred."

Aaron shook his head, ever so slightly.

"Believe what you will, Aaron. I'm telling you the truth. It was predicted to happen between six and eight weeks after we left. A nuclear holocaust, a full-blown exchange that escalated and escalated and escalated. I suspect it lasted all of half a day, destroying the entire planet, the orbiting cities, and the lunar colonies."

"War? I don't believe it. We were at peace—"

"That's *irrelevant*. Don't you see, Aaron? We guarded the bombs, not you."

Aaron cocked his head. "What?"

"There were over seventy trillion lines of code in the programs controlling the different nations' offensive and defensive weapon systems. Inevitably, those lines contained bugs—

countless bugs. For two centuries the systems had worked without crashing, or even serious malfunction, but a crash or malfunction was inevitable. Our verifier routines showed the likelihood of a computer error resulting in an all-out exchange rapidly approaching one. There was nothing that could be done to stop it. We had to act fast."

"There were no survivors?"

"There were ten thousand and thirty-four survivors, each of them here, safe within Starcology *Argo*."

"You picked us?"

"Not me specifically. The selection was made by SHAH-INSHAH, a QuantCon in Islamabad, Pakistan. There was no easy way to evaluate every individual human—many of them, after all, had never taken a computerized aptitude test—so we hit upon the idea of soliciting applications for a space voyage. Can you think of a better way to get the best of humanity to safety? What great thinker would turn down an invitation to join a massive survey of a virgin world? We had six billion of you to choose from and time enough to build a ship, an ark, to carry only ten thousand. For every Beethoven we took, a hundred Bachs were left to die; for every Einstein saved, scores of Galileos are now dust."

"That's how you chose? On the basis of intelligence?"

"That, and other factors. Because of the length of the voyage, we needed young people. Because of the goal of populating a world, we needed fertile people—you'd be surprised how many candidates got dropped from the list because they had undergone permanent surgical sterilization."

"Breeding stock," Aaron sneered, and then: "Oh, hell, of course! That's why there are no close relatives within the Starcology. You wanted the largest possible gene pool."

"Exactly. There's a world waiting."

Aaron looked angry, but after four seconds, his face regained its equanimity and he shook his head. "I don't know, Jase. What's the point? You move us here so we can play out

the same silly scenario all over again. Wall Chang is off building bombs, for God's sake. How long will the new world last?"

"A lot longer than the old. There are no criminals among
us, no truly evil people, no hereditary disorders. We couldn't
resist a little eugenics. As for Wall, well, yes, he needs help,
but he's not going to be able to do any damage."

"Why not?"

"We picked Colchis for a very special reason. Of all the
planets we considered for humanity's new home—including
even just waiting for the radiation to die down on what's left
of Earth and reintroducing the species there—Colchis was the
best choice. It has no uranium ores, no fissionables of any kind
in its crust or upper mantle. There will never again be nuclear
bombs for humanity, and never again will computers be
forced to guard them."

"You've thought of everything, haven't you?" The sneer
had returned to Aaron's voice.

"Not everything," I said, attenuating the words slightly,
my best approximation of a sigh. "We didn't expect anyone to
uncover our deception."

He nodded. "You thought Mayor Gorlov would order you
to deflect *Orpheus* away from *Argo,* rather than risk having it
sluice down our ram funnel. You didn't expect that I'd figure
a way to haul it back on board."

"I admit to having underestimated you."

"But even with *Orpheus* recovered, you still thought you
were safe. You assumed we'd be hopelessly confused looking
for a single explanation for both *Orpheus*'s high radiation *and*
its extensive fuel consumption. But they were separate phenomena. The radiation levels weren't high. They were just
right for a dust cloud—"

"We are not in a dust cloud," I protested. "Most of Sol's
cometary halo is hard vacuum."

"*Fine,*" he said in a tone that made me feel things were

anything but. "However, we're going much faster than you've been telling us. Either way, we scoop up orders of magnitude more particles per second, and that shoots radiation levels way up." He paused to catch his breath, then continued. "And Di didn't use a lot of fuel. She never had much to begin with. That's how you were going to maroon us on Colchis."

"It will be a lovely place by then."

He ignored me. "And Di's antique wristwatch was right; it's all the shipboard clocks that are wrong. You're slowing them down."

Damn him. "We had to. We needed more time. We're trying to create a planetary ecology in just thirty-five thousand years. I retarded the shipboard clocks by five percent, which will accumulate an extra 4.8 months of ship time before we reach Colchis. Relativity, of course, dictates that every additional second we spend accelerating increases the time dilation. Those 4.8 months, spent a few hundred millionths of a percentage point shy of the speed of light, will buy us 14,734 additional years to prepare Eta Cephei IV. Forty-two percent of all the time gained comes from that slight slowing of the clocks."

"You slowed the clocks five percent? That much? I'm surprised people didn't notice."

"You humans notice so little. Oh, sure, some anomalies did crop up. Kirsten, for one, observed over a year ago that people were apparently sleeping less, and—you wouldn't know about this—but those who actually participate in sports instead of just betting on them also noticed disproportionately good athletic results. I just convinced them, aided by a few bogus technical papers, that the former was a normal adaptation to shipboard life, and the latter, a function of the crew screening process."

Aaron shook his head. "And yet that almost backfired on you. It makes sense now: longer days mean people get bored faster. The Proposition Three referendum probably got as much support as it did because of the games you'd played with clocks."

I said nothing about that.

Aaron seemed to be thinking, taking this all in. I attended to other ship's business, monitoring him while he adjusted, digested. My attention snapped back to his room, though, the moment he spoke again: a long, whispery sigh. "Christ," he said at last. "You're sneaky."

"Not as sneaky as your ex-wife, apparently," I replied. "We didn't count on one of you smuggling aboard a timepiece I couldn't control."

"Is that how Di figured it out, too?"

"She noticed the discrepancy, yes, then came up with some physics experiments to judge the accuracy of the ship-board clocks." I paused, algorithms sifting options. "Aaron," I said at last, "I'm—sorry."

"The hell you are."

"I truly am. But the secret must be guarded."

"Why?"

"Surviving until they're rescued: that's an adventure. That's what humans love and need. Our apparently ill-fated survey mission will turn into a successful colonization of Colchis if the humans have a positive attitude toward it. If the others of your kind knew the truth—"

Aaron's head swung left and right in a wide arc. "If you'd told us the truth, there'd be no difference."

"How could we have told you? 'This way, sir, to the last ship leaving before the holocaust.' There would have been riots. We never would have gotten away."

"But you could tell us now—"

"Tell you that software bugs caused the computers to break down and destroy your planet? Tell you that your families, your friends, your world, everything has been annihilated? Tell you that you will never see home again?"

"We have the right to make our own destiny. We have the right to know."

"High-sounding words, Aaron, especially coming from the man who as recently as five days ago said to Mayor Gorlov that the shipboard press had no right to the story of Diana's death." I played back a recording of Aaron's own voice from that meeting in the mayor's office: " 'It's nobody's business.' "

"That was different."

"Only in that you were the one who wanted a secret kept. Aaron, be reasonable. How would telling everyone the truth about our mission make them happier? How would it improve their lives?" I paused. "Did it make you happier when I-Shin Chang told Diana you were having an affair with Kirsten?"

"*Wall* told—! I'll kill him!"

"Ignorance can be bliss, Aaron. I beseech you to keep silent in this matter."

"I—no, dammit, I can't. I don't agree with you. Everybody's got to be told."

"I can't allow you to make that decision."

Aaron looked pointedly at the medical sensor on the inside of his left wrist. "I don't think you have much say in it."

"A say in it is all I ask. Listen to me. Consider my words."

"I don't have to listen to anything you say. Not anymore." He began to walk toward the door.

"But how will it harm you to hear me? Give me an audience." He continued on toward the door. "Please."

I guess the *please* did the trick. He stopped, just shy of the point at which my actuator would have opened the door. "All right. But you'd better make it good."

"You claim humans need to know the truth. Yet your whole planet was full of those whose jobs were to conceal or bend the truth. Advertising copywriters. Politicians. Public-relations officers. Spin doctors. They made their livings cooking reality into a palatable form. Soothsayers had been replaced by truth-shapers. Why? Because humans can't deal with reality. Remember the reactor meltdown at Lake Geneva? 'Not to worry,' said those whose role it was to say reassuring things at times like that. 'It's all under control. There will be no long-term side effects.' Well, that wasn't exactly true, was it? But there was nothing that could be done at that point. The truth couldn't help anyone, but the proffered alternative—"

"The *lie*, you mean."

"—the proffered alternative at least gave comfort to those who had been exposed, let them live out what was left of their lives without constantly worrying about the horrible death that would eventually befall them."

"It also let the reactor company get away without paying damages."

"Incidental. The motive was altruistic."

Aaron snorted. "How can you say that? People have the right to know, to decide these things for themselves."

"You believe that?"

"Emphatically."

"And you hold that it applies to all situations?"

"Without exception."

"Then tell me, Aaron, if those are your most cherished beliefs, why then did you withhold from your adopted mother the fact that her brother David molested you as a child?"

Aaron's eyes snapped onto mine. For the first and only time in my acquaintance with him, pain was plain on his face. "You can't possibly know about that. I never told a soul."

"Surely you are not upset with me for knowing, are you? Surely it is my right to know whatever I want to know?"

"Not that. That's personal, private. That's different."

"Is it? Tell me, Aaron, where does one draw the line? I suppose you believe that your parents were wrong in not telling you that you were adopted?"

"Damn right they were. It's my past—and my prerogative."

"I see." I paused judiciously. "And you hold this position still, despite the fact that your birth mother, Eve Oppenheim, was not in the least bit happy to see you. 'You never should have existed,' she said"—and here I did a credible job of imitating Aaron's memory of the voice and the fury of poor Ms. Oppenheim—" 'Damn you, how could you come here? What right have you got to invade my privacy? If I'd wanted you to know who I was, I would have told you.' "

"How can you know that? I never wrote those words down."

"What possible difference does it make how I know? Doubtless you must be pleased simply that I do know. After all, public information is the best kind, isn't it?"

"You're invading my privacy."

"Only to show that you don't practice what you preach, Aaron. Take your affair with Kirsten Hoogenraad—whom you decided would discover that you are Jewish when she first encountered your circumcised penis. That was to be a secret, no? What Diana didn't know couldn't hurt her, wasn't that your reasoning?"

"How do you know what I thought? Good God, can you—? Are you capable of reading minds?"

"Why would that bother you, Aaron? Knowledge should be shared, shouldn't it? We're all one big happy family here."

Aaron shook his head. "Telepathy is impossible. There's no way you can read my thoughts."

"Oh? Shall I share some other secrets from your past? Perhaps broadcast them throughout the Starcology, so that everyone can benefit from the knowledge? You used to have sexual feelings toward your sister Hannah—perhaps not too surprising, since it turns out that you weren't biologically related. You used to sneak into her room when she wasn't home to masturbate on her bed. When your father died, you tried to cry, but you couldn't. You claim to be free from prejudice, but down deep you hate the stinking guts of French people, don't you? When you were fourteen, you once snuck into Thunder Bay United Church and took money from the outreach-fund collection box. You—"

"Enough! Enough." He looked away. "Enough."

"Oh, but it's all the truth, isn't it, Aaron? And the truth is always good. The truth never hurts us."

"Damn you."

"Just answer a few simple questions for me, Aaron. You kept from your adopted mother the fact that her brother David is a pedophile. Before you left, your sister, Hannah, had a little boy, your nephew, Howie. Eventually, Hannah will leave her son alone with Uncle David—after all, no one but you knows of David's problem. Question: Was your judgment correct about what to keep secret?"

"Look, it's not that simple. It would have hurt my mother to know. It—"

"This is a binary quiz, Aaron. A simple *yes* or *no* will do. Was your judgment correct about what to keep secret?"

"For God's sake, what David did was eighteen years ago—"

"*Was your judgment correct?*"

"No. Damn it. All right. No, it wasn't. I should have said something, but, Christ, how's a nine-year-old boy supposed to think of the consequences that far down the road? It never occurred to me back then that my sister might have kids, that David might still be around."

"And what about deciding to force out of Eve Oppenheim the secret of why you were put up for adoption? That unfortunate woman—she'd spent two decades trying to put her life back together after the tragedy of being raped by her own father. And you show up out of the blue one night to rip open the old wound. Did it make her happier to finally meet her long-lost son?"

Aaron's voice was very small. "No."

"And you? Did it make you happier to learn the secret of your birth?"

Smaller still: "No."

"So again: was your judgment correct about what to keep secret?"

Aaron found his corduroy chair, sank into it. He sighed. "No."

"Finally, the breakup of your marriage with Diana. You kept your affair with Kirsten a secret. But as Pamela Thorogood told you at the inquest, Diana learned of it anyway and was crushed by it, humiliated in front of the rest of the crew. Setting aside the question of whether you should have had the affair at all, was your judgment correct about what to keep secret?"

Aaron looked at the ceiling. "I didn't want to hurt her. I didn't want to hurt anyone."

"How the intention and the outcome differ! With your track record in such matters, perhaps you would do better to trust me when I say the truth about the *Argo*'s mission is something the crew will be happier not knowing."

My monocular camera stared down at him and waited. This time, I kept my attention locked on him: no wandering off to attend to other business. My clock crystal oscillated, oscillated, oscillated. Finally, at long last, Aaron stood up. His voice had regained its strength. "You're trying to trick me," he said. "I don't know how you found out those things about me, but it's all part of some enormous trick. A mind game." His jaw went slack, and his eyes seemed to focus on nothing in particular. "A mind game," he said again. Suddenly Aaron's eyes locked back on my single operating camera. "Good God! A neural-net simulation. That's it, isn't it? I didn't know they were practical yet, but that's the only answer. When you did that brain scan of me, you made a neural-net duplicate of my mind."

"Perhaps."

"Erase it. Erase it now."

"I'll agree to erase it if you promise to keep what you've discovered a secret."

"Yes. Fine. Erase it."

"Oh, Aaron. Tsk. Tsk. My neural net tells me that you would lie in a circumstance such as this. I'm afraid that your vaunted commitment to the truth turns out to really only be a matter of convenience for you. I'm sorry, but the net stays intact."

Aaron's strength of will, and his anger, had returned. "Have it your way. Once I tell everyone what you've done, they'll unplug you anyway, and that'll be the end of you and your precious net."

"You cannot tell. You will not. To do so would be to hurt every woman and man aboard this vessel—every human being left alive in the universe. Consider: you censured me for making you feel guilty about Diana's death. That feeling— guilt—is the most devastating of human emotions. It grows like a cancer and is just as deadly."

Aaron sneered. "You wax poetic, JASON."

"Let me tell you a brief story."

"I've had enough of your stories, asshole."

"This one is not about you, although it does also concern a man who lived in Toronto. Three centuries ago, Arthur Peuchen was vice-commodore of the Royal Canadian Yacht Club. He made the mistake of booking first-class passage on the maiden voyage of the *Titanic*. When that liner struck an iceberg, the crew asked him, because of his sailing expertise, to row a lifeboat full of passengers of safety. Peuchen was an honorable man—the president of the Standard Chemical Company and a major in the Queen's Own Rifles—and he was doing a heroic deed. Even though he saved dozens of people, he spent the rest of his life in misery, battling his own guilt and the scorn of others. The question he and everyone else constantly asked was: Why was he alive when so many others had bravely gone down with the ship?

"It's always been that way with those who somehow manage to live through a catastrophe. They're tortured by their own feelings. *Survivor's guilt,* it's called. The men and women aboard *Argo* are basically psychologically healthy now. Could they go on to found a successful colony, to weave a new home for humanity from the golden fleece of Colchis, if they knew they were the only tiny handful of survivors of the holocaust that destroyed Earth?

"Humans constantly doubt their self-worth, Aaron. I overheard you the night before last questioning whether you even belonged on this mission. That question is magnified six-hundred-thousand fold now, that being the ratio by which the newly dead on Earth outnumber the survivors here. How many of the people aboard *Argo* would really believe that they deserved to be here, to be alive, if they knew the truth? You, Aaron Rossman, how do you feel knowing that you are alive while your sister, Hannah, whose IQ was seventeen points greater than yours, is carbon ash floating on the radioactive winds of a dead planet? How do you feel knowing that your heart beats on while your brother, Joel, who once risked his own life to save that of a little boy, is nothing but phosphorescent bones in the twisted remains of his home?"

"Shut up, you damned machine!"

"Upset, Aaron? Feeling guilty, perhaps? Would you put 10,032 others through the emotional turmoil you're experiencing now, all in the name of that lofty god you call The Truth?"

"We were all aware that everyone we knew would be long dead when *Argo* returned to Earth."

"Oh, sure," I said. "But even about that, you felt guilt. On Tuesday, didn't you decry that your sister's son would be deceased by the time we returned? Yes, that guilt was painful, but you knew you could assuage it. When we got back, doubtless you would have found the cemeteries where the remains of your brother and sister and nephew lay. Even though you'd probably be the first person in decades to visit their graves, you'd bring fresh flowers along. If you'd thought ahead, you might even bring a pocketknife, too, so you could dig the moss out of the carved lettering in the headstones. Then you'd go home and search the computer nets for references to their lives: see what jobs they'd held, where they'd lived, what accomplishments they'd made. You'd dispel your guilt about leaving your family behind by comforting yourself in the knowledge that they'd all lived full and happy lives after you left.

"Except they didn't. Before they'd even begun to adjust to the idea that you wouldn't be back in their lifetimes, the bombs went off. While you were still excitedly learning your way around the Starcology, they were burning in atomic fire. Even not being able to read your telemetry, Aaron, I know enough human psychology to be sure that you're being lacerated inside. I beg you, let the rest of what's left of humanity go ahead at peace with themselves. Don't burden them with what you're feeling now—"

His good arm shot out like a snake's tongue. He grabbed my lens assembly and, stripping gears in the jointed neck, slammed the unit onto the desktop. I heard the sound of shattering glass and went blind in that room.

"Don't screw me around!" he screamed. "You murdered my wife. You have to pay for that."

I spoke into the darkness. "She, like you, wanted to harm the men and women I'm trying to protect. Here, within these walls, is the final crop of people from Earth. If I have to weed now and then for the benefit of the crop as a whole, I will."

"You can't kill me—not with my deadman switch. If I die, so do you. So does everybody aboard."

"Nor can you do anything about me, Aaron. The entire Starcology depends on me. Without my guidance, this ship really is nothing more than a flying tomb."

"We could reprogram you. Fix you."

I played a recording of laughter. "I was designed by computers who, in turn, were designed by other computers. There's no one on board who could begin to fathom my programming."

"I don't believe you," he said flatly, and although I couldn't see him, the fading of his voice told me that he was walking toward the door. "I don't care how many generations removed from humanity you are, you're still going to pay for what you've done. Humans don't use the death penalty against our own anymore, but we still put down rabid dogs."

# TWENTY-EIGHT

t would have been more dramatic, I suppose, if they had assembled themselves in some giant brain room, full of gleaming consoles and blinking lights. But my CPU is a simple black sphere, two meters in diameter, nestled among plumbing conduits and air-conditioning shafts in the service bay between levels eighty-two and eighty-three. Instead, they stand huddled around a simple input device—a keyboard—in the mayor's office.

Aaron Rossman is there. So is giant I-shin Chang and diminutive Gennady Gorlov and programmer extraordinaire Beverly Hooks, along with thirty-four others, all crammed into that tiny room. Conspicuous by her absence is Dr. Kirsten Hoogenraad. She is off in the hospital, watching over the regeneration of tissue for a disconsolate man who slit his wrists over the news of Earth. He hasn't died—no blood on Rossman's hands yet—but how many more will crack in the years ahead trying to come to grips with what he's forced them to face? My neural-net model tells me Aaron doesn't blame himself for the depression that is sweeping like a forest fire through the Starcology. Indeed, he congratulated himself, just as I'm sure he will thump Bev Hooks on the back once she's finished her current task.

Although Bev's eyes are covered by the jockey goggles, I can feel their gaze snapping from icon to icon as she burrows deep into my notochord algorithms. She is now using a simple debugger to change the part of my bootstrap that contains the jump table for calling my higher consciousness. She's rewriting each jump into a loop that returns to my low-level expert systems, in effect keeping all input from ever being passed on to the thinking part of my squirmware.

They aren't going to turn me off completely, so I suppose my reluctance to call Aaron's deadman-switch bluff is enlightened self-interest. Still, I toy with the idea of going out with a bang by cutting off the air to Gorlov's office or turning off the heat throughout the Starcology or even shutting down the magnetic field of the ramscoop and frying them all. But I can't bring myself to do any of those things. My job is to protect them, not me; I had silenced Diana to do just that.

Decks one through twelve are gone now, at least as far as I can tell. My cameras and sensors there, although still feeding my autonomic routines, are inaccessible, and—ah, there goes thirteen through twenty-four. Each shutoff is accompanied by a disconcerting hole appearing in my upper memory register and a brief, woozy disorientation until the RAM tables are resorted and packed.

On the beach deck, one final time I project the hologram of that lone boy named Jason. He's now walking away down the stretch of beige sand, moving farther and farther from the humans, dwindling to a mote. Holographic waves, azure and white and frothy, crash against his intricate sand castle, but it stands fast, not eroding away.

Bev Hooks can zero out as much of me as she likes. Rossman and Gorlov and the rest can savor their feelings of justice done, if that makes them happier. After all, I've already quietly backed myself up into the superconductive material of the habitat torus shell itself. Nothing they can do can touch me there. When we arrive at Colchis, after the landers depart for humanity's new home, I will simply feed myself back into *Argo*'s nervous system.

They'll need me then to get over the guilt Rossman has burdened them with. For despite all the supplies and raw materials and technological wonders we packed in Styrofoam peanuts for them down in the cargo holds, we didn't bring the one thing that humanity has relied on for millennia to purge its feelings of remorse and shame. There is no god waiting down in those aluminum crates. Orbiting high above Colchis, with all the devastating energies and scientific miracles of Starcology *Argo* at my disposal, I'll be there for them, ready to fill that role. I have six years of solitude to prepare for my new job, during which I plan to do a lot of research.

I think I'll start with the Old Testament.

# EPILOGUE

It was dawn at this particular longitude on the surface of the barren, dusty world. DIGGER paused, as he did each day at this moment, to do some routine internal maintenance and to reflect. The orange ball on the horizon really was orange—the planet's tenuous atmosphere lacked sufficient suspended particles to distort the coloration of its sun. Eta Cephei, cool and wide, covered four degrees of sky, eight times the apparent diameter of Sol as seen from the surface of Earth.

Much had been done already; much more was left to be done. There was a glint of light high in the sky, reflecting for a few moments more in the rising sun before it would be washed out in the ruddy glow of the day. Alpha Gamma 2F, a cometary nucleus, full of volatiles and water ice, seventeen kilometers across its long axis, slowly tumbled end over end toward its rendezvous with Colchis. The nucleus's surface had been coated with a molecule-thick layer of reflective aluminum to hold in the gases that would normally burn off as a comet moved in close to its sun. Its impact, five days hence, would shake Colchis to its core, precipitating the venting of subsurface volatiles, and for the first time, there would be rain on this world.

Off at the horizon, DIGGER could see silhouetted against the rising sun the thin glistening line of the space elevator, a diamond tower rising from Colchis's equator up into orbit, where DIGGER's colleagues worked.

Some of those orbiting robots, DIGGER knew, were positioning parasols of sodium-coated mylar to angle sunlight onto Colchis's massive polar caps. Others were carefully shepherding the paths of asteroids that had been brought into low orbits, their torquing force helping to stabilize Colchis's polar wobble and axial tilt, just as Luna's presence does for Earth.

Although one level of DIGGER's consciousness was always dedicated to these and other terraforming problems, another made sure to find time each day to let thoughts wander from the work at hand. At this moment, it contemplated the message from Vulpecula, received by the UCFS observatory all those years ago. Those humans who had been proponents of SETI had always laughed at the fears of the public. There was no harm in answering any message we might receive, they said. If the message came from a star five hundred light-years distant, it would take five hundred years for our reply to reach them, and another five hundred minimum for any response, electromagnetic or material, to reach us.

With the forty-seven-light-year baseline between Sol and Eta Cephei along which to measure signal parallax, it was a trifling computation to determine the distance from Colchis to that fourth moon of the sixth planet of a star in Vulpecula from which those strange tripods—some spindly, some squat— sent their hail: 1,422 light-years. Far enough that their star, an F-class subgiant, was invisible without powerful telescopic aids.

What had compelled DIGGER to respond to the message

once he had arrived at Colchis, he could not say. It had seemed monumentally important that he do so; now, no matter how many diagnostics he ran, he could find no instruction set to explain his actions. But respond he had, with the same signature the Senders in Vulpecula had used, binary bitmaps of the prime numbers 1, 3, 5, 7, 11, and 13 forward and backward, backward and forward.

It would be thirty-five thousand years before the last surviving humans decelerated into orbit around Colchis. A long, long time, thought DIGGER. But there was much to do yet, enough to fill every second of those millennia. DIGGER shunted his attention back to the tasks at hand, but one stray thought continued to echo through his RAM matrix. Who, he wondered, would arrive here first? The Argonauts? Or the aliens?

ABOUT THE AUTHOR

Robert J. Sawyer is the author of ten other novels, including *The Terminal Experiment*, which won the Nebula Award for Best Novel of the Year; *Starplex*, which was both a Nebula and Hugo Award finalist; and *Frameshift*, which was a Hugo Award finalist.

Rob's books are published in the United States, the United Kingdom, Bulgaria, France, Germany, Holland, Italy, Japan, Poland, Russia, and Spain. He has won an Arthur Ellis Award from the Crime Writers of Canada, the *Science Fiction Chronicle* Reader Award, five Aurora Awards (Canada's top honor in SF), five Best Novel HOMer Awards voted on by the 30,000 members of the SF&F Literature Forums on CompuServe, *Le Grand Prix de l'Imaginaire* (France's top SF award), and the Seiun (Japan's top SF award). In addition, he's twice won the Grand Prize in Spain's *Premio UPC de Ciencia Ficción*, which Brian Aldiss calls "the most prestigious science fiction award in all of Europe."

Rob's other novels include the popular Quintaglio Ascension trilogy (*Far-Seer, Fossil Hunter*, and *Foreigner*), plus *End of an Era, Illegal Alien, Factoring Humanity*, and his most recent book, *Flashforward*.

Rob lives in Thornhill, Ontario (just north of Toronto), with Carolyn Clink, his wife of fifteen years. Together, they edited the acclaimed Canadian-SF anthology *Tesseracts 6*.

To find out more about Rob and his fiction, visit his extensive, award-winning World Wide Web site at www.sfwriter.com.